LOST AND LOVED

KATHY JO BUTLER

BALBOA.
PRESS

A DIVISION OF HAY HOUSE

Balboa Press books may be ordered through booksellers or by contacting:

Balboa Press
A Division of Hay House
1663 Liberty Drive
Bloomington, IN 47403
www.balboapress.com
1 (877) 407-4847

Because of the dynamic nature of the Internet, any web addresses or
links contained in this book may have changed since publication and
may no longer be valid. The views expressed in this work are solely those
of the author and do not necessarily reflect the views of the publisher,
and the publisher hereby disclaims any responsibility for them.

The author of this book does not dispense medical advice or prescribe the use
of any technique as a form of treatment for physical, emotional, or medical
problems without the advice of a physician, either directly or indirectly. The
intent of the author is only to offer information of a general nature to help
you in your quest for emotional and spiritual well-being. In the event you use
any of the information in this book for yourself, which is your constitutional
right, the author and the publisher assume no responsibility for your actions.

Any people depicted in stock imagery provided by Thinkstock are
models, and such images are being used for illustrative purposes only.
Certain stock imagery © Thinkstock.

Print information available on the last page.

ISBN: 978-1-5043-2875-3 (sc)
ISBN: 978-1-5043-2876-0 (e)

Balboa Press rev. date: 04/07/2015

Dedicated to those that stood by me, gave me encouragement, love and support, Thank you : Pam, Mary, Sue and my brother Steve that is living proof love can make you strong no matter what life hands you.

CONTENTS

Chapter 1   Lost 1
Chapter 2   Dreams 9
Chapter 3   Sam 15
Chapter 4   Brian 21
Chapter 5   Hospital 24
Chapter 6   Waiting 26
Chapter 7   Awaken 33
Chapter 8   Fragile 37
Chapter 9   Recovery 42
Chapter 10 Home 47
Chapter 11 Bonding 51
Chapter 12 Hypnosis 57
Chapter 13 Discovery 62
Chapter 14 DNA 68
Chapter 15 Megan 72
Chapter 16 Memories crash 76
Chapter 17 Nicolas Stephen 82
Chapter 18 Spring brings beginnings 85
Chapter 19 Burn 89
Chapter 20 93
Chapter 21 Hunt begins 98

Chapter 22 Protection 101
Chapter 23 Z 106
Chapter 24 FBI..109
Chapter 25 Plan 114
Chapter 26 Fighting Back 116
Chapter 27 Final plans 120
Chapter 28 Million dollar prize 124
Chapter 29 Closure..132
Chapter 30 Wedding day..136

CHAPTER 1

LOST

She could hear a muffled voice asking "miss, are you ok", as she felt someone gently shaking her shoulders. She tried to open her eyes she felt like there were pounds of sand gluing them shut. Miss, Miss his voice raised up in urgency. With every ounce she had, she forced her eyes to open, slowly, a slit at first allowing bright blinding light seep in, jolting a pain inside her head. A soft moan escaped out of her mouth and she began to blink and forcing her eyes to focus. She saw the outline of a man, leaning towards her miss, are you ok? Inside her mind, she responded with I don't know, but she could hear a muffled slur of her words. Her throat was raw and dry, and her voice cracked as she tried to speak. The man helped her to sit up. He had a cup of water and told her to sip slowly the coolness of the water trickled down her throat, quenching the rawness, the room seemed to spin and nausea hit her sudden and swiftly. She tried to take deep breaths to help her to clear the fogginess she felt. The man was kneeling in front of her. She could feel him; smell the blend of aftershave, sea salt and manly sweat. She felt oddly comforted to have him there, to catch her if she began to fall. Miss, he said. We'll be docking soon. Let me help you up, can I call someone? The world seems to stop swimming before her. She tried to comprehend what he was telling her. Docking? She looked around. It seems she was on a boat of some kind. Boat? How did she get on this boat? Where was she? She placed her hands on his shoulder. Can you help me stand? She asked weakly. Her feet planted on the hard ground, the boat rocked and she felt she was rocking in rhythm with it. The man hands were tightly around her waist and she fought to find her balance. She closed her eyes and just focused on holding on, the man suggested to help her to the ladies room. One foot in front of the other, he said, let's walk easy, easy now. He kept saying over and over. Inside somewhere her body was responding to his orders and her legs moved with every command. They found the ladies room, he walked her to the sink. In front of a mirror, she saw a figure unrecognizable. Ragged, unkempt hair, black circles darken beneath her blue eyes. Bruises around her neck, head and hands. Her shirt was ripped and disheveled. Dried blood and dirt streaked the front of it. Miss he said, I need to go, but I want to help you. Is there anyone I can call? What is your name? She stopped staring at herself. She forgotten he was in the room with her. She turned to look at him. No she whispered, there is no one. My name is Brian, he said, he smiled and tried to sound calm and chipper, but she could see his horror of her appearance in his eyes. I am ....I .....She stopped. The words wouldn't come out of her mouth. She didn't know who she was. She started to panic inside and she gripped the sides of the sink. Closing her eyes she tried to remember. My name, my name she kept saying to herself. The problem was nothing was coming to her. She didn't know. Well miss, the horn blasted on the ship. The ferry is docking in 5 minutes. You cannot stay on board. I can help you make it off the ramp but that is as far as I can go. Where are we? She asked. ….why Friday harbor he said. I hate to rush you we only have a few minutes. He handed her a backpack, said here are your things. I will be outside waiting for you. The green pack was worn and fray around the edges. It was canvas and soft, a keychain of silver angel wings hung on the flap. She touched it. It didn't feel familiar. She opened it up. Inside she found a pair of jeans, a bright pink hair brush, a white tee shirt and an oversized blue button man's shirt. She pulled it out and looked at it. On the front pocket a faded name patch was sewn on. The name Nick in red letters was all it said. She dug some more, opening the zipper pockets, she found some keys and a small black leather wallet. She opened it. No identification, no credit cards. Just a stick of gum and a roll of money wrapped tightly in a rubber band. She could hear Brian knocking, urging her to hurry. She quickly steadied herself. She still felt nauseous and a pain in her right temple, she pushed this away and began to run the water. She washed her face, brushed her hair and changed her shirt. She was in so much pain, it hurt to move her muscles and her arms felt heavy and uncoordinated. As she disrobed she saw her ribs red and purple with bruises. A cut that was scabbing over lay jagged over her right breast. The view was horrifying. She pushed back tears that sprung to her eyes. Not now she said, not now. She pulled on the white tee with effort. Her arms were scratched and since she wanted to try and keep stares and unanswered questions from strangers, she put on the work shirt as well. Looking the best she could, she threw everything back into the backpack went out the door to meet Brian and preparing herself to what she might to find in this Friday harbor and to figure out why she is there and more importantly, who she is.

It was warm beautiful day in normal circumstance. But it wasn't normal for her. She made her way down the ramp and found an empty bench. Her legs were wobbly and ached. She found it hard to maneuver and every ounce of her will didn't seem to be enough to make her body cooperate to do what she needed. .She sat down hard. Felt the hard wood against her back and butt. A cool breeze tickled across her face, reminding her that she had open wounds. Hands shaking, she decided to try and eat. She opens the sack lunch and pulled out the sandwich, a business card was tucked inside the wrapper. Squinting, she read Brian McAdams, Port Authority, and Friday Harbor. (360)555-5555 on the back he hands wrote; please call me if you need anything. Go see Chief James, he's a friend.

She had a pit in her stomach. She didn't remember her name but she knew intuitively to be very cautious of men. But for whatever reason, she couldn't bring herself to throw away the card. She tucked into her jeans and decided to finish her lunch and then go find a place to stay.

She felt a bit better except for the pounding inside her head. She decided that she would first find a store to get some supplies. A general store was not far in the distance. She saw a large hand painted sign and bright colored flags flying, flapping in the wind, calling customers to come and visit. Once inside, she was overwhelmed by the fresh warm scent of coffee, cookies baking and there in the corner was a huge display of chocolate delights! Rows of clothes, sweat shirts in all colors, with logos of dolphins and whales, advertising "welcome to Friday Harbor", jewelry made by local artist swung from hangers on a shelf and fun stuff animals of sea turtles and star fish.

She could hear the customers talking and from most of the conversation she listened to, most of the patrons were local residents mixed in with tourists asking for directions.

As she smiled and thinking of getting some caramels, a little boy around 5 or 6 came up to her.

"Hey lady," he said, "what happened to you? Did you get into a fight? Or an accident? Billy in my class, he fell off the jungle gym and he got a big bruise like you on his face!'

She was mortified. She had forgotten what she must look like. And now, it seemed the whole store was staring and wondering about her and what may have happened

She was paralyzed as she didn't know how to respond to this much inquisitive little boy.

"Alex," yelled his mother from across the store, "mind your manners and leave that lady alone"

Alex, not deterred from his mother's rant, kept going on, he was for some reason fascinated by the lady with bruises. He moved from looking at the bruises to the faded name written across her shirt.

"Hey lady", he said again," you're wearing a boy's name." Why are you wearing a boy's name?"

Before she could respond a little girl Alex's older and much wiser sister of about 8yrs came over. Stop it stupid she scolded. Mom says to come over here now.

No, he said, she's wearing a boy's name.

The little girl stopped, looked at the name tagged, scrunched her face in deep thought. "Hmm," she said, "I think it's not a boy's name but it's missing a letter, I think her name is Nicki"

"No", argued the boy," it's Nick, he's in my class, and I know that named." "It's a boy, she's a boy."

The girl looked at her brother, then back at the lady." Is your name Nicki she asked?"

She looked at the children." Nicki"? Well why not. She needed a name however temporary, so all she could think of was to nod her head at the little girl.

Smug and satisfaction spread over the girls face. See she said to her brother. And then promptly grabbed his shoulders and both walked away.

She, aka Nicki, paid for her stuff and walked out of the store. She felt more tired and ever in need of a place to lie down. Standing in the street, she looked up and down, there on the side of the road a few steps away a sign said INN.

A blue building that resembled a 1940's house sat on the edge of the road. A white picket fence and arbor lined the manicured lawn. Bright yellow daisies in the flower bed and over flowing pots of lavender stood on the porch. A cute hand painted sign of the word INN hung over the red door and a small sign in the window saying rooms available.

Nicki walked in. the door swung open with a sound of a bell as she stepped across the threshold. A small braided rug in shades of green was in the front area, deep shades of dark mahogany desks and in the waiting area was couches of deep brown leather, rustic lamps and a huge fire place. Behind the desk a girl around the age of 18 was on the phone to her friend as they were quickly making plans when she got off work.

Nicki walked up to her, the girl signaled with a finger to give her one more minute before hanging up her call. Nicki stood, reading the local pamphlets and saw a newspaper lying on deck. H headlines about a missing lady from Clark County Washington. As Nicki went to grab the paper the girl was finished with her call.

Can I help you? She asked.

I, I need a room Nicki said.

Sure said the girl, I am Sarah, I would be happy to help you do you have a reservation?

No, she whispered. She felt tired and defeated and it was all she could do was to keep the conversation going. It's been a long day and she just wanted to lie down.

Its ok, she was chipper and sweet. We have rooms available. Now, do you want a queen, smoking or non?

Sarah seemed to go on and on about the room. Nicki couldn't follow along to what she was saying. She tried to focus but it was getting harder and harder. All of the sudden she was brought back to attention as she heard Sarah ask her name.

I um, I am Nicki. Nicki Clark.

Clark, the name of the county the lady was missing. She didn't know why she chose it, it was just there and easy enough to "borrow" a made up name.

She paid for the room, a week was shown how the TV worked, no room service but there was delivery from a local diner, wake up calls were available, towels, toiletries and if she needed anything else, someone was always at the desk 24/7 the chipper Sarah said.

Nicki thanked Sarah, shut the door and locked it. Not feeling secure, she pushed the side chair next to the bed up against the door too. Slowly, she stripped out of her clothes, turned on the shower to hot and stepped inside.

The steam and sprays splashed against her battered body. The soap stung as she washed the dried blood away and she cried. After 20 minutes of water and suds, she decided she was ready to leave it and lay down. Drying off, in front of the mirror, she closely examined her body. Her stomach and chest was cut and bruised, her right thigh was all bruised and upon

Further examination, her head wasn't as bad as it look previously. It was a bump and the open gash looked like it was already scabbing over.

She wrapped a towel around her. This was enough for one day. She saw a coffee pot in the corner and made a small pot of hot water for tea. She pulled down the bed and crawled in.

That was the last thing she remembered as she fell off to sleep

CHAPTER 2

DREAMS

Nicki tossed and turned. Images swirled in and out of her dreams. Some faces so clear she could touch them others dark and blurry. She felt fear and woke with her heart pounding and sweat pouring down her body.

She was stiff and sore. For a moment, she felt she was just having a bad dream but as her eyes focused on the darkness, she saw she was in a lonely room, foreign to her and no closer to knowing who she was or how she got there.

She looked to see the time from the bedside clock. Its numbers glowed in the dark with hues of red burning from its face. 2:00 am. Sadly, she didn't know the date. She laid there. Normal things came to her, she knew the sound of rain that she should brush her teeth etc. but she had no memory of her or anything before yesterday.

She thought of the ferry, the man that helped her. She wondered how long she was there, where she boarded. She decided to get up, she still had the towel wrapped around her, and she got up and went to the bathroom. She found a robe hanging behind the door and slipped into it. She washed her face. The bruises are turning to the yellow gold and hints of black. Her eyes still seemed sunken and really nothing she could do to make it better. Glancing around the room, she saw her green bag. She decided to dump it out and take a better look inside. Perhaps there was some clue to this all.

Turning on the light, she dumps the backpack out onto the bed. Opened up all the zippers, slid her hand inside to see if there was anything. Sure she had everything out; she started to examine the contents.

She found the wallet, the money, a pair of jeans, a hair brush. A pair of silver hoop earrings and a necklace, a blue oval pendant with a white angel on it.

She counted out the money. Surprisingly she had over 3000 dollars. Where did it come from? She doesn't feel she would steal it, maybe she saved it? All she knew was it was a lot of money and she had to save it to live off of and figure out the answers that is missing.

She picked up her stuff and started to put it back into the pack grabbing the jeans she decided she would wear them and find out if the inn had a washer to clean the other ones she had on. As she started to fold the jeans up she felt something in the pocket. Reaching her hand in, she found a ring and a match book. The ring was a single diamond on a gold band. She felt no attachment to this ring, but somehow she knew it was hers. She looked at the matchbook, on the cover was a name "Blackout". On the inside was a number written in ink.

She didn't know why, but this matchbook made her stomach hurt. She got immediate butterflies and nausea started to set in. Panic, shear and utter panic but why?

Rain started to tap the windows as she sat on the bed. She went to pull back the curtains and saw the raindrops and puddles glistening showing the reflection of the street lamps. Everything was so silent. Just the rain, it was peaceful and she began to breathe to rhythm of the drops hitting the window and calms herself. She needed to have a plan. She told herself that in the morning she would go out and find a notebook, pen, and make a plan. She would go out to the ferry and see if there was a schedule and a map to find out where she may have come from. She started to feel better, she would find out who she was, and she would survive. There was a reason for her to be there at Friday harbor, she will explore to find out why, and maybe there is someone that knows her. Maybe tomorrow she would find out everything. She started to smile and decided to crawl back into the covers and sleep.

She woke hearing the soft knock of maid service. Looking at the clock it was 9am. She stretched, rolled out of bed and pulled on her jeans and tee.

Throwing her hair up in a pony, brushed her teeth, she decided to go out and get breakfast while the maid cleaned up her room. Grabbed the backpack, she headed for the street. The rain stopped but the scent of it lingered with the puddles. It was also cold and she knew the tee shirt wasn't going to be enough. She headed for a diner, and then she would do some light shopping. Finding a table at the local diner was difficult. They were slammed but she managed to find a spot at the bar area. The food was amazing and she was starved. She kept to herself, she was aware of the stares and what people must be thinking she just wasn't ready for questions that she hadn't any answers for. She ordered the house special, eggs toast hash browns, sausage juice and coffee and she didn't leave a crumb. She felt refreshed and although she was still sore and battered, she felt much better and stronger than the day before. She left a tip and went out to find the supplies she needed. First stop was coat or sweatshirt. She found a cute store just opening up and bought a deep blue hoodie sweat shirt. It had a small dolphin on the left upper side with the words Friday harbor underneath. She also bought a new tee, baseball hat; some make up, notepad, pen and a lightweight navy blue zip up jacket. She also then bought some energy bars for later and on her way out, a newspaper. She pulled on the hoodie, it was soft and warm it was a bit big but it covered her nicely and she could pull the hood up if needed more coverage, but for now she decided to put on the cap and pull her pony thru the back again, this helped hide the bump on her head and shade her bruised eyes.

Tucking her supplies in her bag, she grabbed the newspaper and folded and placed in the zipper part of the bag and headed for the pier.

Her first goal was to find a schedule and map of the pick-up points and times of the ferries. The pier was already busy, hustles of people boarding and unloading the ferry. Cars lining up waiting their turn to pull onto the lower deck as pedestrians waiting to walk on board. There was a booth to purchase tickets and she walked up to that. She felt that is where the schedule would be and perhaps a helpful person to direct her better. As she neared, she stared out to the water and watched the ferry churning water as it lie in dock. She heard laughter and noise of people chatting in all directions overwhelming her as she waited to approach the booth. Then out of nowhere, she saw a man, tall big shoulders and greying hair and she began to shake. The man didn't see her but she froze watching him, he was in a yellow slicker and smoke from his cigarette billowed out of his mouth as he was talking to another man. She watched him, fighting the feeling of fainting. She started to shake but she couldn't make her legs move. The man turned, looked straight at her and began walking towards her. Her throat felt raw and dry. Burning but she couldn't speak. The scream was stuck somewhere inside between her chest and throat, nearer and nearer he walked, she closed her eyes and she could hear the swishing of his pants and the crunching of his boots as it hit the wooden dock. Closer, she could smell him. Spinning and spinning her head was throbbing, vomit coming up and she couldn't stop it. Then, in a blink he walked right past her. She put her hands on her knees and lowered her head. Breath she commanded herself, breathe. She opened her eyes, letting the focus come back and slowly raised herself up right. The man was behind her, she could see him, hugging someone, back slapping another and chatting like nothing was amidst. He wasn't for her. But now she had a clue of sorts. There was a man like this that made her fear.

Fear wore her down. Her mind told her there was nothing there but her body wasn't listening. She trembled and hated that she was scared, alone and lost even if she was on a pretty island surrounded by the soothing sea.

She stood for an hour on the dock, waiting for her nerves to calm. Exhausted, she went back to her room. She had forgotten about the maps.

Running, she was running. She could hear sirens in the distance, the street was narrow, an alley, bricked walls surrounded each side and she could smell garbage, she tripped and hit hard on the road bits of gravel stuck to her palms and knees. A noise was behind her, sounds of glass breaking and heavy footsteps coming faster, she could hear breathing, she dragged herself up, her heart pounding, her breath echoing inside her head making it hard to hear clearly, someone yelled, she screamed. Nicky sat up, dripping with sweat, someone pounding on her door. She was disoriented, another nightmare so real she felt she her hands raw and throat hurt from her screaming. She got out of bed, grabbed a robe and opened the door. The night clerk was there. "Miss' he said, the neighbors heard you screaming, are you ok? I called the police."

Nicki stared at the night clerk; standing behind him was a tall man, about 6 feet, broad shoulders, and sandy hair. He wore a white shirt and jeans and a gold badge pinned on his left breast pocket.

"Miss", I am Chief James.

CHAPTER 3

SAM

Middle of nowhere New Jersey. That is what they called his little town. It was a small community and on his street everyone knew each other. He loved his street. Houses with porches each had its own color and garden in front. Big maple trees lined the streets and sidewalks always filled with walkers, skaters and the occasional chalk artist, painting tic tac toe or drawings in pastels pinks and blue.

Every kid on nowhere lane played at each other houses, all but Sam's. Sam and his brother, and three sisters kept friends out of their home. They would spend time with the neighbors; Sam would mow the lawns of most every house sometimes bringing Billy his kid brother with him to rake. His sisters Joan and Katie would babysit on an occasional Saturday night. His sister Megan was just a baby barely a year old trying to learn to walk. each sibling taking turns to watch her and making sure she was fed, never to cry.

On weekends, Sam stayed with his best friend Johnny. Johnny's mom would always bake cookies and his dad would teach them how to throw a curve ball and sometimes even coach a game or two. Those were his best days, but not today. Today was July 4, 1976 and Sam was 14. It was going to be the best day! The neighbors on this momentous occasion was throwing a block party, even his father was home from work and was in a great mood. His mother helped set up and even provided a cake made especially for Sam. Yep, today was going to be the BEST in history, he could feel it in his bones!

Dusk fell and bobs were lit. Smells of charcoal and hot dogs filled the air. Large ice chest overfilled with sodas and beer, tables covered in checker cloths lined up with mounds of homemade goodies and food. Sparklers lit, lawn chairs spewed everywhere, neighbor ladies gossiping of latest this or that and men talking shop.

Voices, laughter, dogs barking the noise and excitement were contagious and everyone was waiting for fireworks that promised to be fabulous.

Sam and Johnny ran to the end of street. An evening game of baseball, friends gathered, Johnny pitching, Sam at the plate.

Sam leaning back, waiting for that perfect pitch, low and outside. He gripped the bat, watched as the ball was coming towards him. Spinning, twirling, humming as it was making its way to the catcher's mitt. And then CRACK, Sam swung. He heard the bat hit the ball and in that instant moment, he knew he hit a home run. They all watched as the ball went higher and further out, GONE... Sam relished the groans of his team mates as he rounded the bases, each step on the bag a celebration …yes it was the best day. As he was heading for home, he heard a loud BANG. It shook the air and he swore he felt the earth trembled. They all stopped, first instincts was to look up, maybe fireworks were being shot off, that Sam thought would be priceless, a celebration of his home run, but he was shaken out of his trance, sirens blaring and lights flashing as they shot down the street passed him. His friends all threw their mitts and starting running, crowds were forming and all seemingly in front of his house. He wanted to run, his legs felt like rubber and for a brief moment he was paralyzed. Sam, summoned strength to get to his house. He saw his baby brother on his knees, pounding his fists on the ground, his sisters were huddled, being soothed by Johnny' mom. He felt he was in a fog, making his way thru the crowd in jelly. He heard "always knew it" and "it was a matter of time", murmurs being said as he past the faceless people. He couldn't comprehend everything, it was all so surreal, and then he saw. His mom, on the ground. An ambulance attendant over her, he could see Crimson red blood covering her golden hair as they covered her face with a white sheet. Sam looked for his father. He was there, disheveled, looking like he aged in a moment 10 yrs. his white tee shirt red and dirty. He was being handcuffed and gave a look over to Sam; he only nodded as he was put into a cop car.

His sisters and brother each went to a different home, he was too old so stayed in juvenile places until at age 15, he ran away, hitchhiked to Seattle and stowed away on a ferry boat and landed on Friday harbor.

Sam has been on the island now for 36 yrs. He became chief for the last 25 and at 51; he is still strong, athletic and respected by everyone. He stood tall at 6 ft. dark salt and pepper hair. He had blue eyes and a scar about 2 inches, right across his chin.

He was a hell raiser at age 15, got caught stowing away from Mr. Bob McAdams, ferry captain. Bob was a big burly man with hands size of mitts and one hand on Sam bony 15 yr. old shoulder, Sam knew he couldn't escape. Sam was taken to live with the McAdams, they had a son Brian a few years younger and for reasons that escape Sam to this day, Bob and his wife took him in as their own.

Sam grew and learns the island. He cleaned up his "attitude" out of respect for his new family and only fought when it was really really necessary.

He always defended the weak being picked on and maybe out of memory of his mother, he made sure no girl or woman was ever abused in his presence.

He learned he had an aptitude for the law and after graduating early; he went to Seattle police academy, learned and worked his way up to detective, homicide and SVU, (special victims unit) for raped and abused children and women mostly. He would go back and forth on the ferry to see the McAdams and one day, Bob became ill, Doris his wife of 49 yrs. passed 3 weeks before, Sam was worried and on a spring day, 4 weeks later on what would have been their 50th wedding anniversary, Bob passed away.

Brian and Sam buried Bob scattering his ashes on a lonely ferry ride from the island to Anacortes. They drank a beer, shed a tear and at that moment, Sam decided to quit SVU and become the local chief on the island.

Sam immediately knew that look. That hallowed eyed fright or flight and he swore he could feel her heart beating straight out of her chest from where he was standing. He knew a lost fragile woman when he saw one and was certain he didn't make any sudden moves. He kept his voice in soft monotones when he introduced himself and looked straight into her deep blue eyes as he watched them tear up and heard her voice tremble.

He introduced himself; I'm Sam James, Ma'am, and Chief of police here on the island. As he took off his hat and stepped forward, she fell. Plop, straight to the ground.

Sam rushed forward. Same time pulling his one way calling dispatch, Janie, call ambulance, got a female unresponsive at the inn.

Crowd gathered while EMTs lifted the unconscious fair hair lady on the gurney. Whispers and rumors began to rumble around, drugs, one said, big party someone else said. Sam paid no attention to nonsense and nosey busy bodies of the island looker loos. As she was taken away, he met with Sarah, the inn keeper, gathered her name as Nicky Clark, and arrived barely 3weeks ago. Pays by cash, quiet, polite, keeps to herself and spends most of her time at the docks looking or waiting for someone.

He looked around in her room. Nothing much. She was neat, carried only a backpack, a few items, toiletries and a few change of clothes and cash. To Sam, this was a sign of someone on the run and in trouble or running from it. By the looks of her and the way she responded of seeing him, he'd say she was running from it. He started to pick up a pair of jeans lying on the floor and underneath he found a folded business card. He opened it up and read his name and number on one side and on the other was his friend's Brian business information.

Grabbing the card, Sam went off to the hospital to check on Nicki Clark and on his way call Brian to find out more about this lady and the mystery surrounding her.

CHAPTER 4

BRIAN

With dark Irish good look, black wavy hair, deep blue hair, Brian McAdams was a handsome man Rugged, hands that showed years of callous hard work on high seas, stubble chin that covered a slight dimple when he smiled. A crooked grin that drove women crazy and a build proven to his favor in close calls aboard the ship. Most times Brian was a friend to everyone, but he was also feared by those who crossed him as he also had a reputation for quick fists. He took his job very seriously and worked extremely hard to achieve the all of his accomplishments. Brian was smart, quick wit; He could quote famous poets, philosophers as well as recites the stats from the latest major league baseball players. He graduated high school early, top of his class, had scholarships and offers to any college of his choice Yale, brown, Harvard, but the sea was his calling and the law like his father, and he didn't want to stray far from it.

He was born and raised on Friday harbor, the only child to loving but strict parents and when he was 4 his parents took in a boy of 15 to live with them. Sam James. Sam was a confused, rambunctious, smart mouth teenager and often pushes his parents to the brink of patience. But Sam was never awful or unkind to Brian. He always had time for him, he played with him, taught him to play ball, even taught him how to drive at 15, and have his first beer with. Sam was Brian's idol and there wasn't anything Brian wouldn't do for him, especially now that his parents were both deceased, Sam was the only family he had.

Brian was out at Seattle port when he got an urgent message to call Sam. At first his stomach knotted, Sam doesn't ever call unless it's really drop everything important. So, that was what Brian did. No need to call back. Dropping everything, he hopped the ferry back and sailed back to Friday's port to see the urgency.

Standing on the deck, the ferry slowed to dock. Brian watched the island come into view. Doesn't matter how many times he came home, this sight of seeing the homes in the back drop of deep green pine trees and deep blue sky, takes his breath away. The smell of clean, crisp air, fresh pine and scents of lavender that filled the air just luring him home. He closed his eyes and just drank it in and sighed. The pang of his parents not being there to greet him still pained him but he knew their spirit still lived there and he was comforted by this.

All of the sudden he was happy to be home and couldn't wait to get off the boat. It's been months since he's been back and been at the old house and was glad that for whatever urgency Sam may have that called him here.

The horn sounded, the ferry rocked and hit the side gently rocking as it becomes tied down. Sides open up and guard rails down and Brian makes his way down the ramp to head for the police station to find Sam.

CHAPTER 5

HOSPITAL

It was like drowning she supposed, she could hear but she couldn't open her eyes and then she would go under and be sucked deeper and deeper into sleep. At one point she heard beeping and swishing of machines, murmurs of people speaking in the distance, then nothing. Utter silence. She was in another place, like above watching down and seeing a home movie of herself. Evening at a beach, the moon so full that lite the beach with its brightness. She wasn't alone. She was with two other females. Sisters. She wasn't sure how she knows this but she is sure of this now, these ladies are her sisters. They are in long flowy skirts of different shades of blues and greens. One had hair of dark brown, wavy and long to her waist, flowers were woven in a wreath and she wore in on her head. The girl had blue eyes and looked to be younger than her. She held a candle of bright pink and stood with her and the other sister in a circle on the beach. The other sister had reddish hair curly; she was taller and older than the two. She too had blue eyes and she smiled at them both. She was saying something a chant of sorts as they faced each other in the cool sand. She watched them, the sand, the moon, the candle, the chant. It seemed so normal, so familiar. So real.

She knew the words; she knew what was supposed to come next but how? She knew there was to be a symbol to be drawn in the sand that was next, a protection. They were saying speaking. She was straining to hear, she wanted to hear, it was so foggy, and it was so hard she was too far above them, she was too weak to see and they were not speaking loud enough. She was frustrated and tried to move closer but she was restrained. She kept trying but feeling pulled back, the beeping making interrupting the chant, she wished it would stop so she could hear them. She wanted to ask them who she was. She reached then she awakens.

She opened her eyes. Tubes in her nose, mouth, she couldn't speak and to her left she saw a glass bottle hanging from a metal stand. The beeping noise coming from a monitor beep louder and louder above her head. Swish of her blood pressure cuff taking readings every few minutes going on, squeezing her arm relaying the digital readings to an electrical stand next to her bed. Her head hurt and her eyes were blurry, but she tried to focus as someone hovered over here with a light shining in her eyes.

CHAPTER 6

WAITING

Sam stood by her bedside and watched her for days, struggling inside her deep sleep. Something about this lady ate at him. Stirred a knot inside his stomach and he felt for some reason beyond himself to protect her. He kept watch as nurses came in and out, checking her vitals and changing tubing and handing new bottles of liquid as it pumped into her blood. He waited as orderlies wheeled her in and out of her room taking tests and x-rays. He inquired to doctors as they consulted as to what was wrong with her. And to best of each their knowledge, they didn't know. She seemed not to want to wake up they said. There wasn't a physiology reason for her to be under for so long. Nothing they can explain. All they can do is waiting.

So Sam did. He waited and watched. He heard her murmur and watched her eyes flutter. He wiped her brow when it started to sweat and he held her hand because he didn't know what else to do. He held the business card that had his name on it in brain's writing, turning it over and over. Brian wanted him to see her. Help her. He needed to know why. He knew instinctively she was in a lot of trouble and he had to reach Brian.

Sam headed for the exit of the hospital to stretch his legs and make another call to Brian. The sun was setting and the glare of the light hit his eyes, temporarily blinding him to seeing anything outside. He raised his hand to shield, casting a shadow across his face. Locals saying hello as they passed him, some saying he looked tired. Some just a wave and a nod. He felt tired. His body was stiff from sitting so long and a pang of guilt from shirking other duties and focusing so much time on this one lost soul. He should just file a report, wait until she wakes and let social services help her and move on. But he cannot.

He lifted his radio, called the office. Nothing earth shattering to report. Fender Bender outside on Spring Street. Mrs. Porter on the lavender farm reported she heard some noises during the night, a patrol went out and nothing was found. Some visitors got a bit rowdy and fine on lime kiln drinking waiting for the pods to swim by. All in all, life was peaceful and nothing to be worried about and it was hardly noticeable that he wasn't in the office all day. But he was sure tongues are a wagging about him being at the hospital with the total stranger that was now the town's mystery gossip.

Putting away his phone, he saw the swagger before he saw the face. Old blue jeans, same old worn flannel shirt and dark hair blowing in the breeze. Brian was here.

Brian! Sam exclaimed. !

A side crooked grin on spread on his stubble face, "Sam, My brother! How the hell are ya!!

The men locked hands and gave a hug. Been far too long my friend, Sam said, but you look well.

They were genuine happy to see each other., You look tired, Sam. And in need of a cold beer by the looks of you and a steak. Let's go find platter and tell me what the urgency of your call.

The men headed off and smiling and back slapping to the local diner.

Sam ordered two medium well ½ inch thick steaks, fries and salad for both of them and a big tall draft.

The tables were highly polished wood. The grains gleaming with its rich dark colors, nicks and gashes from years of wear only added to the charm and ambiance of the room. The juke box played songs from oldies to country, a tune from up incomer latest idol of some sort winner playing. Chattering filled the room with a vibrating hum, smells of grease and fries permeate the air, Sam and Brian slide into a booth in the back of the room. Waving to the waitress, Sam signaled two fingers and Sally, the owner of the tavern, she immediately sent two tall frosty glasses of beer foam slouching down the side's right in front of them.

Brian stretched his long legs in front of him, kind of made him slouch in the seat. Taking a long draw of beer he studied his friend, his brother across from him. Sam looked tired he thought. More than tired. Troubled. He didn't like this feeling that was creeping inside his gut.

Taking a deep breath, Brian dove in and broaches the elephant in the room.

Ok, spill it he said.

What is the problem that is gnawing at you?

Sam gave a hard long look. He knew he couldn't ever keep anything from Brian and one thing he always could count on was directness.

Ok, Sam said. He reached into his pocket and pulled out the worn business card that had his and Brian's name on it.

Brian, took it, looked at it, and with puzzlement he looked back at Sam and shrugged. Ok? It's my card so?

Yes, Sam said with my number on the back

Yeah? Brian turned it over. Hmm I don't recall where'd ya find it?

Sam, said, there is this lady, went to call on her at the Inn, she fell unconscious and now in the hospital. I found this on her.

Brian stopped for a moment. OH he said. Pretty girl bout 35 or so?

Ya Sam said.

Ya, and with that, Brian went on to tell Sam about finding her on the ferry, her being battered and bruised. Dirty and couldn't remember her name. He tried to help her and how she refused, and the only thing he could think of to do was to give Sam's name and number to her and urge her to seek him out.

As Sam listen, his gut clinched. His hair on the back of his neck sprang to life and prickly feeling came over him. He knew there was more to this story and he knew deep down this girl was in trouble, no danger. She was in danger. He felt it. He didn't realize he was gripping the mug of beer so tightly as he intently listen that his big hang actually crushed the glass and it shattered all over the glossy table. Beer dripped thru the cracks and onto the floor and almost onto Brian's lap.

With disgust in him and frustration, Sam lost his appetite and stood up. He threw two twenties on the table ran a hand thru his hair and headed out the door.

Hey,,, Sam, wait...Brian jumped up and grabbed Sam's shoulder.

Sam, c'mon what is it, tell me? What is with this girl that has you unnerved? Do you have the hot's for her a sly grin came onto Brian's face.

No, Bri, Sam said. I don't know what it is. I feel it deep in my gut, there is trouble coming and it surrounds this girl. As for love, she's a bit too young for me and that isn't it at all, although she's really attractive, I feel that she is vulnerable, lost and beaten. I feel someone did a real number on her mind and soul and isn't finished yet.

Brian let out a deep breath, Man, he said. I kind of knew it. Look Sam,

I am here for a few days, let me help you track this down, if there is a problem coming I want to be here too next to you to fight it.

Sam, turn gave Brian a shake of the shoulder and for the first time in days, his stomach relaxed a bit and he even let himself smile.

Thanks Bro, now I need a shower and some sleep; let's meet up in the morning. And with that the men parted ways, the rain began to fall and a cold shiver ran up Sam's spine, but he knew it wasn't because of the wind.

Restless, he stared at the digital hands of the clock turn second by second, by 2:3o am he felt it useless to try and lure himself to sleep. The rain still falling gently keeping a steady stream outside his windows. Shirtless, shoeless, he made his way to the kitchen, brew a pot of coffee and open the patio door. The freshness of the rain, the quietness of the village gave him a sense of peace. He loved this island, the people he grew to know all these years. Their families, the newcomers, the friendly waves and helping hands when a neighbor needed it. The trust they bestowed in him, a rough kid from nowhere, they embraced and loved. He took a deep breath, it felt like it's been so long since he exhaled and breathed. He was rarely off his game and rattled by a case or anything for that matter and this stranger, had he unnerved. His mind wandered a bit to his mother, his sisters, his brother, the hole inside began to ache and he started to curse himself for letting himself go back to them. He knew he had the resources now at his disposal to find them, but why would he mess with their lives. When he was younger he fantasized of a reunion and how happy they would all be, but the past was painful enough and opening that wound would probably only bring heartache on what he hoped were lives fulfilled with joy. He always said silent prayers for them, and hoped they too remembered him. And like a beacon the buzzer went off his pager and he was snapped back into reality. He rushed to get it, slammed into the corner of the wall...... mother fffffer ....ugh....hopping on one foot he leaped across his bed found the pager and dialed the phone it was the hospital.

This is Chief James,

Chief, this is Nurse Janie Mills at Peace. Dr. Simpson left orders to call you once the patient Ms. Clark was awake. He's with her now and would like you to come by after his rounds at 7am to see him at his office.

Tell the doc, I'll be there.

As he hung up the phone, Sam felt dread and elation at the same time, perhaps now the puzzle can be put together and some answers to questions he has. He knows she's under no obligation to speak to him, but he was going to give all his persuasive power to convince her to let him help her.

CHAPTER 7

AWAKEN

She could see the light in her eyes. She tried to shield it away but her arms were too heavy and uncooperative, they wouldn't move to her face. She tried to closing her eyes tightly, squinting out the light that was now like a laser to her brain causing a headache to form.

She heard the voice before she saw his face.

Miss he said. Miss, hello miss,

I am Doctor Simpson. Can you tell me your name please?

He spoke with a funny accent she couldn't place. His voice was nasal like, high almost feminine but not. She tried to speak but there was something blocking her throat and mouth...

Oh shhh shhhh, sorry miss, sorry. Ok you have a tube he said my sorry. I am going to take it out at you, understand, and nod your head

He spoke fast and quickly she had a hard time absorbing his words while she wanted to nod he was already hovering over her and saying ok one two three breeeeeeeeeeeeeath and with that he pulled out the tube she started coughing, someone helped her to sit up and the room spun a little, the voices told her to breath and it would be ok her throat felt on fire, raw, sandy. She could see everyone now, people in white coats machines beeping around her, talking to each other as if she wasn't there.

Ok, said the doctor, as he looked into her eyes again with that light.

I am going to leave you only for a moment, the nurses are going to help you get changed and clean up, I will be back to talk to you.

Ok? As he squeezed her arm and headed out the door.

She was then wheeled into another room, she was helped to bathed and given ice for her throat. They gave her a new gown and white comb to brush her hair. A large cotton swab was to be used as a makeshift tooth brush and for a moment she was given a hand held mirror.

The face wasn't familiar, she looked more hallow and thinner. On her wrist was a plastic band, tiny print with F, Clark, and Nicki DOB unknown.

How long have I been here she asked the nurse as she dressed?

Oh honey, I think about 5 days now.

5 days she whispered.

Now, don't worry honey, Doctor will talk to you.

Taking you back to the room.

She was in another room; it was light blue, single bed with matching spread on it. A metal side table and a small window. It was more cheerful than the other room, tiled floor in big black and white check patterns there wasn't any big beeping machines but oxygen tank on the wall, a TV in the corner and a big wipe able board underneath with nurse's name on it.

She was helped into bed, side rail up, given a call button and shown how to use it if she needed anything. More ice chips on a tray and a TV remote. And with that they left her and she was alone.

It felt like hours she was there counting the spots on the ceiling, trying to remember how or why she was there. Still trying to figure out who she was. The name on the armband was as foreign as a language to her. She was frightened, alone, unsure where to go or what to do. Who can she trust? Should she trust? She needed answers that she did know how to get them is another thing.

The door swung open. A little man of stature, about 5'6, unruly curly brown hair that seem to shoot in all directions, black wire framed glasses and a white coat that looked too big and hung below his knees.

He was quick moving and starting chatting the instant the door open.

Ok he said, ok now, can you tell me where you are?

In a hospital

Good good, now how did you get here?

I don't know

Do you know what happen to you before they brought you here?

No

Is there anyone we can call for you?

No

Where do you live?

I …ii….am staying at the inn

How long have you been here on the island?

Um….what day is it?

Sept 24th

About a month

Where were you before the island?

I don't know

Miss, he said do you have any memory of things before you came here?

No

Is your name Nicki Clark

I don't know.

With that, he walked closer, looked into her, e yes, took a stethoscope listen to her chest. Tested her reflex, and with a slight smile.

Said, now don't worry. I did test, everything is normal. We will find out what is wrong.

Why can't I remember she ask weakly?

You will, in time you will. Just rest. I will give you something to rest.

And he left the room.

CHAPTER 8

FRAGILE

Walking down the corridor, he could hear the overhead pages for medical personnel, buzzing lights of patients needing assistance. It was still early, but the hospital was in full operational mode. People in the waiting room, pacing for the outcome of loved ones, some waiting their turn to be seen for this or that ailment. Sam ignored it all; he looked for the arrowed signs pointing him to the office of Dr. Simpson.

As he was making his way, he saw the little wiry man, hair a muss, white jacket too big for his little body, wrinkled like he slept in it all night. Glasses a skewed and he was mumbling into a tape recorder. Dr. Simpson looked up, waved and motioned for Sam to follow as he continued to talk in rapid tones, spouting medical terminology that Sam didn't understand.

His office was beige, small and over crowded with furniture and books. A large desk took up most of the room and made Dr. Simpson look even smaller sitting behind it. Mismatched chairs of greens and blues were for visitors, one covered in magazines. There was one window overlooking the parking lot and a ledge that held a plant desperately needing watering.

Sam felt awkward and closed in this room as he patiently waited for the doctor to finish up. He tried to sit and fidgeted with his hands, picking imaginary lint from his jeans, losing himself into thought.

Simpson snapped the recorder, ok, Chief or Sam, which do you prefer?

Sam came to attention, Sam is fine he said.

Ok, good, well, let's talk about Ms. Clark shall we?

Sam nodded.

Well, normally, I wouldn't be speaking to you at all, confidentiality an all that, and I was fully prepared to say this to you yesterday,

Sam, stated to interject but was waved off., Dr. Simpson continued in his fast speaking manner,

However, this case is unusual. Looking at this girls scans, x-rays, labs, etc. she was normal, no reason for her to become unconscious and remain that way for 5 days. But, her x-rays showed a lot of abuse. If I didn't see the patient first and was just shown the x-rays, I would have said this was a victim of torture.

Sam, stomach knotted and his throat became dry. He was clinching his fist without being aware of it. His mind started to swirl and anger began to creep up. He did his best to keep even keel and not let it show.

So, Doc, did she say what happen?

No Sam, that's the other part of this unusual case. This girl has no memory. She doesn't know how she got here, who she was or where she came from. Her name isn't or very well couldn't be Nicki Clark.

Sam was lost for words. He blew out a breath. And ran his hand thru his hair.

Doc, what do we do?

Well, Sam, she needs help, care and a lot of it.

Do you think she would talk to me?

Yes I do, she wants to know who she is, but she is fragile and this will take a lot of time and patience on your part, you must follow my instructions and when I say it's too much you will have to back off. The mind is a tricky thing, and she can revert more if we are not very careful and be lost inside maybe even forever.

Ok doc, when do we begin?

Well Sam, I feel you need to start by gaining her trust. Not a lot of questions at first. Get her to know you and be comfortable around you to open up.

Ok, Sam whispered.

Tell me when can I start?

Give her a day. She needs a day to adjust being coherent and alert, I want her stronger too.

Ok, in the meantime, I can start doing some digging around here.

I don't think you will find a lot Sam; the answers are locked inside her.

Well, Sam said, I have to start somewhere., And with that, he stood, shook the doc's hand, "Let me know how she is doc, I will be back tomorrow" with that, he turned and headed out the door. His mind racing on a game plan, he decided to call Brian and update him on everything.

Calling Brian on his way to the station, he asked him to drop by later and to bring dinner. Right now it was barely 9 am and he needed to go in and see his much neglected staff. First, he would stop and buy a dozen of donuts to soften the blow of him being away.

6pm came soon enough, he finally finished up the last stack of paperwork, signed off traffic citations and reports of summer incidents that has come and gone. End of September, the last of tourist go back to wherever they come from, leaving the occasional last minute vacationer to take advantage of the island goods before it too shuts down and prepares for winter.

Brian sauntered in and saying hellos everyone and hugging Anne, Sam's 80 year old secretary that keeps him and the office in order. She's known Brian since he was born and gave an affectionate scolding for not coming to see her more often.

Burgers and cold fries, Brian plopped the bag and himself on Sam's desk.

This is dinner?

Beggars can't be choosey he smiled.

With a growl in his stomach and loud groan, Sam opened the bag and grabbed the greasy but delicious sandwich. He was hungrier than he thought, taking less than a minute to woof it down.

She also was getting to know Sam; he would come by, take her outdoors and have lunches or dinner, never probing to0 much, but was kind and fatherly to her.

He said he would help her; all she had to do was to talk to him. She believed him she didn't understand why, but she felt she could trust him, feel the protection he exuded. She didn't know much, and a part of her wanted to know why she was there, and really who she was. But her nightmares reminded her that she might have to face something horrible and evil, the dread of that kept her silent and would only nod to Sam and say I'll think about it

Sam dropped by for his usual visit. In his way of thinking if she got used to seeing him, she would be less frighten and start to open up to him. Today, he stopped and picked up a pizza, a six pack of cola and for desert chocolate chip cookies from the local bakery.

He found her in the atrium, picking leaves from the patio lemon trees; he watched as she closed her eyes and inhaled the scent of citrus. A small smile crossed her lips, the look of pleasured innocent, savoring every last drop of essence. He didn't want to interrupt, he stood quietly, letting her have her moment.

She opened her eyes; she was still smiling and the shock of being watched spread over her face. Embarrassment flushed her cheeks and instinctively she took a quick step back.

Sam! I was just um, sorry didn't hear you.

You looked so peaceful I didn't want to disturb, you, he tried to brush it off as lightly as he could. He didn't like the way she was already fidgeting her hands and stammering.

The serenity of her face instantly became fright; paleness took over as her color began to drain.

Keeping it light, he walked over to the flowers, bent his big body to smell a rose,

Lovely, he said, someone can really get lost in smelling this. No wonder women love them, he smiled

She blew out a breath, and tried to stop wringing her hands. Ya she said, they are lovely. You know this is lemon verbena, the scent is light citrus and if you boil the leaves in water,rinse your hair, it helps improve the circulation of the scalp as well it makes a wonderful soap and tea with mint.

He just stared at her. He didn't realize she knew what she just said. As she tumbled the words out and held onto the leaf of the plant she stared at him, suddenly realizing,

Oh MY...I don't know how I know that but I know that....I know plants, herbs, it feels so natural!

He smiled. A memory! It wasn't much but it was something and d it gave him hope that more will follow.

You had a memory! Now that is awesome, and was truly happy for her.

She was laughing, her eyes shined in amazement, like a child seeing their first Christmas tree.

Now, let's go celebrate with this pizza and then we can tell Dr. Simpson. With that they headed outside to sit on the grass and. celebrate the victory of remembering.

Discharge day came. Nicki was really nervous. She dressed in the jeans and island sweatshirt that Sam brought by a few days before.

She lost her room at the inn and in Sam's usual calm, reassuring manner, told her not to worry. At the urging of Dr. Simpson, She was to begin the following week seeing a psychologist to undergo hypnotherapy. It was felt that if she was taking back under hypnosis she would be able to open the lock door inside her mind.

She worried about what she may learn, it was becoming easier to be Nicki, and she was even starting to create a past by making it up and to start to plan a future here on the island. What if what she remembered took her away from all of this? But she logically knew she had to face the fears and find out truly who she was.

She gave permission for Sam to run finger prints into a system that finds missing people. He even suggested a DNA test just in case it helps locate someone and verification of family if should they ever find anyone.

Packing up what little she had in the room, the nurse came in with a wheel chair and papers to sign her out of the office. She had orders she said to take her to the front entrance and they were to wait.

Wait? Wait for what? She asked.

The nurse shrugged and said she didn't know, just following orders.

Climbing into the wheelchair she felt awkward and guilty.

I can walk; really, this is silly to push me

No this is hospital rules. Need to take you clear to the doors to ensure your safety.

As the big sliding glass doors opened, she saw with great surprise Brian and Sam with huge silly grins, standing there with balloons of bright blue, reds ad yellow ad one big blue teddy bear.

The sight of them big manly men holding a bear made her giggle. She was as surprised as she jumped out of the wheel chair not waiting for the nurse to stop. She couldn't help herself throwing her arms around both men.

Oh My Goodness! You shouldn't have!!

Both men laughed, Brian was visibly blushing when Nicki planted a kiss on his cheek.

Sam bowed and said you're chariot awaits my dear, motioning to the red jeep parked next to him. They were all laughing as they pulled away from the curb, a sight to see, two men, a pretty lady, balloons and a big old bear.

CHAPTER 10

HOME

They pulled up to a two story Victoria home. It was white with dark blue shutters. Over grown flowers in pots scattered around with a garden full of lavender. Nicki stared in awe to the beauty of it.

Where are we? She asked

Your new home, Sam smiled.

What? How?

Brian answered; well it belonged to my parents. I own it and hardly ever have the time to be here and take care of it. After talking to Sam, thought it would be perfect for you to stay and help take care of the place.

I ….I …don't know if I can afford this

Oh, don't worry, in exchange for rent, I need a care giver to watch the place, take care of the gardens and you can when able, you can pay for your own food and utilities. There is a little studio out back, and that is my place. From time to time, I will be staying there when I come home.

She stood dumbfounded. How did this luck come to her? How did these two strangers now her friends come to her life to rescue her. A tear started to flow down her cheek.

I don't know what to say, she whispered. I am touched and so very grateful.

Brian smiled, well, you haven't seen inside yet, it needs a lot of cleaning and the gardens need a lot of weeding, so you will have your work cut out for you.

She only smiled, I can't wait! And with that, she grabbed the bear and jumped out of the jeep, ran to the gardens.

Inside of the house was just as lovely as the outside. It needed dusting and vacuuming, a woman's touch, but otherwise, it was warm and inviting. The living room was filled with old pictures of family on the wall, black and white photos in dark wooden frames. The couches were cream and blue with oversized pillows of blue, yellows and greens. It had adjoining den with furniture in sheets still covering them, she couldn't wait to uncover and see what treasures held beneath

On one entire wall was a big fireplace of red brick just waiting for a cozy fire to be lit, she could imagine Christmas, hanging stockings and decorations of pine wreaths.

Pale yellow walls and dark wood cabinets adorn the kitchen, white counter tops and copper pots hung from the ceiling. An old 1950 gas stove in the corner. Faded curtains of yellow and little blue flowers covered a big picture window overlooking the back yard gardens. Old flower pots of herbs long dried and dead stood on the sills. Well, she would fix that she thought.

She lovingly went thru each room, seeing in her mind how it would look clean, with fresh flowers in pretty vases and candles.

She loved this house. It felt like she belonged as she went upstairs to find the bedroom. Brian said she could pick anyone she wanted, the first room off the right was his parents, as she came to the door and opened it, she felt it private and somehow would be so evasive if she moved into it, so she just opened the room, walked in. she could smell the faint odors of aftershave and sweet lilac perfume. She could feel in a sense the presence of his parents, so she turned and before she left the room, she said a prayer of thanks to them for allowing her to live in their home, she promised to take care of it, and most of all, thanking them for raising two good men that have rescued her and became her friend.

She chose the room she supposed was Sam's. Smaller than the other two, it was sparsely furnished, the bed was bare and an old dresser with a missing handle stood in the corner. The window overlooked the backyard, it needed curtains and linens, but it felt homey just right for her.

She saw a line of closets in the hall way, she decided to open up and explore. The first one she found had the sheets of various colors, towels and blankets. She chose a light blue set of sheets and found a white and blue comforter and pillows.

The next closet she found old vases, a box that had white sheers, she decided to use as curtains. She found odds and ends of things for the bath, old rugs, lamps etc. It was like shopping in a fabulous second hand store. The items were hardly worn yet had character. She piled things in her arms and went to set up her room.

The bedroom set up to her satisfaction, it looks cheery, except for one thing. Putting her finger to her lips she smiled and ran down the stairs, stopping in the kitchen to find shears. Outside to the garden, she started clipping flowers. She started with the lavender, roses of white, and pink and yellow, she found sunflowers, baby's-breath and some ferns for greenery. Gathering them all up in her arms she knew she cut too much, the fragrance was overwhelming and she couldn't stop herself from smothering her face it all the petals.

It took 3 vases to house her creations. She placed one in her room on the dresser, one in the living room and one in the kitchen. Already, the house looks like home. Her spirit and energy high, she dove into cleaning like a mad woman. She found mops, dust rags, vacuum and began.

CHAPTER 11

BONDING

It was almost Christmas, Nicki been on the island now for 3 months. She, Brian and Sam had now formed a friendship, almost like a family. She was beginning to get more and more pieces of her memory. She still didn't know how she got to the island or why she came, or her name. But little things like she had a knack for baking, gardening, she knew herbs and the medicinal value of them. She was feeling more comfortable.

She decorated the house, in little lights, pine garland with red bows on the stair railing and the mantle. She found red stockings and put Sam and Brian's name on it in glitter. She felt it quirky and maybe a bit tacky but fun. She found old ornaments in the attic and decorated a tree. The house smelled of cinnamon, pine, and the pumpkin candles she lit filled it more with warmth and comfort

Sam called and said he was coming over with Brian. They had some news and ideas to talk over with her. She felt a clinch in her stomach. She knew she had to discuss and face her past. Up until now she was going to her sessions with the psychologist but inside she was content how her life was.

She baked some pumpkin bread. She discovered how baking soothes her as well it kept her mind and hands busy. They didn't knock anymore, the comfort level of their relationship was that they could come and go with ease.

Sitting down to a slice of warm bread and fresh coffee, Brian began;

I found out that you boarded the ferry in Anacortes. I found the video of you alone in the station. I traced you staying at a local hotel the night before. The clerk said you were pretty bad off, wanting to call someone or take you to the hospital, but you said you had already been and showed him a hospital band on your wrist.

The clerk didn't ask a lot of questions but you did say you were in Seattle and was very tired.

Nicki stared blankly at Brian; it was like listening to a story of someone else.

Do you have any memory of Seattle? He asked.

She didn't, but it made her instantly scared when he mentioned it.

Sam, saw the look of panic starting to creep onto her face.

Clearing his throat, he chimed in, ok, well I ran your prints in all the known, there wasn't any hits. I also ran your stats in the missing persons, there wasn't anything either.

Her throat was suddenly very dry and the coffee began to taste like sour acid.

What...does this mean? No one misses me?

Well, he said, it does present a lot of questions. Like maybe you're an orphan?

I don't have one person knowing am not gone? Not one friend? She felt sad and dumfounded.

What kind of person am I?

Look, Sam said, this isn't a reflection of you. It could mean whoever hurt you kept you from your family, there could be a lot of reasons, let's not jump to any conclusions.

Sam, she said, I am lost. Been here for months, and no one, not one soul is looking for me

Maybe, he said, you didn't want to be found, maybe, you ran and made sure that you weren't...

She didn't even consider this. A headache began to creep over her. She got up, cleared the plates, keep her hands busy she thought.

As she went to put the dishes in the sink one fell and crashed she saw the pieces fly and scatter all over the wooden floor. With that, a memory came to her she saw herself falling, glass flying all around her, she sank to her knees.

Brian was the first to see her, jumped out of his chair and ran towards her. She was shaking, hands covering her face.

At first he thought she was cut from the broken dish and was upset it fell, but one look at her closer, he saw it was more, much more.

HEY, he said, what it….instinctively he grabbed her, is she screamed,

And he stepped back, not knowing what to do, putting his hands in his pockets. By then Sam was there, kneeling next to her. Careful not to touch, but speaking in low, soothing tones.

Shhhhhh, he said, it's ok

Breathe, Nicki breathe.

Tell me, tell me what you saw.

At first she couldn't, the words, the air wouldn't come to her, she was stuck, the effort to breath was so much and for a moment she almost forgotten how to.

Then she heard him, she saw into his eyes, help me up she whispered.

He helped her to her feet. Brian stood and watched stomach hurting from the sight of her being so pale, scared and he couldn't help at all.

Sam helped her to the other room, told Brian to get her a glass of water. Sitting on the couch, the warmth of the fireplace, he placed a soft throw over her lap. Brian gave her the water. Now Sam said, take a drink tell me what happened.

She said she saw herself, falling out of a window, glass shattered all around her and she could actually feel how it felt falling, falling.

Was it a memory, dream? He wondered

She looked at him, almost like she could hear his thoughts,

I went out a window Sam, I hit the ground. I know this.

Brian let out a slow breathe. Whew., she looked up at him, saw the concern. She felt embarrass for screaming at him, she knew he was only trying to help.

I'm sorry Brian, I didn't mean anything...

He cut her off before she finished the sentence. Hey, he said, it's ok really it's ok. And he walked over patted her and gave a slight kiss on top of her head.

Sam, told her to rest in the chair. He and Brian walked outside to get more firewood, more so to have a private time to chat.

What do you make of that Brian asked?

I am trying still absorbing it. I can't imagine what she is going through and to see going out of a window, wow, ya know..?

Do you think she was thrown?

What do you thinking Bri?

I don't know, really my mind is a jumble and I know I feel helpless watching her.

Sam looked at his friend, Are you falling for her Bri?

Brian looked to the ground, I don't want to be, Sam.

Sam laid his hand on Brian's shoulder. Just be careful my friend she isn't strong yet

Don't you think I don't know that! I know that. I am fighting this Sam, and this is the first time admitting how I am feeling and I am jumbled about it. I don't even know how you're feeling towards her, I mean; I see how she responds to you and how you are around her.

Sam shook his head. No Bri, I don't have those kinds of feelings, I feel more brotherly I guess you could say. I do want to protect her and help her. Nothing more, She has become our friend and in a sense our family now.

Some reason, Brian felt the constant knot in his stomach begin to loosen. He gave a slight smile. What do we do now?

Well, Sam said, I think she needs to be pushed more to be hypnotized and recall everything. She was pushed, thrown or jumped; in any case we need to help her find out. But I do know this, she has a fear of someone and if they threw her, the may feel she is dead.

Brian gathered some more wood. Handed a few logs to Sam,

Well, let's go back in. And Sam, I want to stay here in the room out back just in case she needs me.

Sam smiled. Ya, Bri…be careful.

CHAPTER 12

HYPNOSIS

Nicki went to the psychologist office. She had asked Sam to come along for support and was grateful that he could afford time away from his job to be there. She knew she was leaning on him a lot and felt a bit guilty for it. The office was bright and cheery, so not as scary as she thought it would be.

Sam met her on the sidewalk outside; he was still in his jeep, talking on his cell. He waved and smiled. She felt instantly relaxed.

He walked over to her, he said that he had to leave and was very sorry but there was a boating accident on the other side of the island and he had to go. Brian was going to come by to sit with her. She was disappointed but of course understood. With that, he gave her a hug and she walked in alone.

The receptionist was a round faced red headed lady; older in mid sixty's with big dangling earrings that was silver Christmas packages. She greeted Nicki, told her to have a seat it would be only a few minutes before she was taken to the back offices to be seen by the doctor.

She was trying to calm the nerves as she wiped her sweaty hands on her jeans. She was having just mixed emotions of excitement of unlocking her memories and fear of what that may tell her.

She stared down at the carpet, mentally counting the strands of green shag fibers. The door opened and her name was called, as she stood to walk back, Brian walked into the door as well. He smiled, and said hey let's go get shrunk....making her laugh ...they walked into the back together.

Dr. Robert Lane, 15 years on the island, at age 45, he was well published on hypnosis therapy and regarded as a good psychologist by his peers. But to look at him, he looked like a senior from high school, a star player on the football team. He had looks, build and youthful big boyish grin and at times his movement clumsy. He was sitting on a big chair of worn dark brown leather. He smelled of old spice. He smiled as Nicki walked in, showed her a chair equal looking as his. Offered her a bottle of water and gave her a moment to relax and settle into their session.

Dimming the lights, Dr. Lane pulled his chair closer to Nicki's he faced her but not so close to violate her space of safeness.

He gently asked her for her hand, on the top of the back of her hand he tapped it three times. Nicki, we are going to make you relax, you are safe, when it becomes too scary or difficult to you, and I will help you wake up out of your relaxed state by tapping your hand like this. But at any time you want to stop, your mind will allow you to come back to the present.

Are you ready?

Nicki nodded yes.

Ok, Count backwards from 10 he instructed.

As she sat in the big comfy chair. His voice quiet, monotone, soothing her. Feel the safety of the chair, the softness as it holds you, you won't fall, y you are safe he said. Listen to the sound of my voice he gently pushed her to go further into trusting him, making her lull into a state of relaxation.

When they got to 1, she was under. He asked her to go back to childhood, told her no fear, no harm would come to her. Go back to a memory. She took him back; she started talking about grass, the smell of fresh mowed lawn, cookies baking and the sound of fireworks all around her. She recalled she was around 1, she then remembered a time around 4 being with her two sisters, and then being taken to another home, not seeing them again.

The doctor then, brought her more present; tell me at 16 he said, she recalled living in many homes many states. One place was in Kansas City where she learned to grow herbs. He gently pushed for names of the people, sisters, herself, but Nicki wouldn't say it. By the time he brought her to the age of now, she began to panic, she recalled being in Seattle, before her heart began to race so badly that the doctor felt it was too much for her, and brought her out of the hypnosis.

Ok, Nicki, one two three, you are in the present. You are safe, you are ok. You will let your mind remember the safe things.

Brian silently sat watching the progression of her, he found himself reliving the moments with her. Feeling the pain, loneliness and abandonment. He was transfixed on her face, the beauty and softness of it, the glow when she smiled and the tears as she recounted her past. His heart ached and soared, he was falling hard for her and it was more than wanting to protect, it was her ways of biting her lip when she was thinking, the hum when she was cooking, her crooked smile and childlike wonder when she saw a dolphin. He was falling for her, and this was new and scary for him. He didn't know how to approach her or tell her, he wanted her to love him, to take his hand and fall into his arms, but she was fragile yet, and he knew she had a past that haunted her, chased her in her dreams. She will need to overcome this and he wants to be there to help her thru it all.

The session was almost ending, he could, at times, hear her voice change, lighter, and sweeter at recalling good times. Dr. Lane or Robert as he insisted to be called, starting to tell her to breath and start to come awake, he was counting again from 1 to 10 telling her she would remember today and that again, she was safe.

Brian was disappointed that her identity wasn't revealed nor what happen to her, but it did give clues she had a family and she was moved around a lot, sounding like she was in in foster care.

Nicki was spent; a slight headache began to form and was a bit nauseated. She felt she was spinning for a long time and then stopped. Robert said it was normal and that it will get better each time she goes under. She was so disappointed not to know her name but was told that will come, give it time.

Brian took her home, made her some lunch and made her go take a nap. Before he tucked her in, she turned and thanked him for staying with her today. She was tired and felt better having him there. He didn't know what else to do, looking into her big blue eyes, sad and lost, he lean and ever so gently brushed his lips against hers. He was surprised she didn't pull back, and he looked down at her, touched her face, brushed her hair away from her eyes, and kissed again on top of her head. She smiled and without words, turned and crawled into bed. This was a weird and exhausting day she thought, and closed her eyes with the feeling of Brian's lips against hers. She would have to talk to him about this later, but for now, she was a bit confused and comforted by him.

He shut the door and blew out a breath. He was kicking himself for that slip of reserve but yet his heart was alive and he could still taste her. Although he couldn't help it, he smiled. He was in love with this lonely girl and the summersault his heart was doing was proof. He would have to think really hard of what to do about it.

Not wanting to stay and await for Nicki to wake, He decided to meet up with Sam and fill him in.

CHAPTER 13

DISCOVERY

Sam was in his office, engrossed in stacks of paperwork on his desk.

He didn't even see Brian walked in and was a bit startled when he plopped down in front of him.

Hey bro, looks like you were in deep thought.

Ya, just focusing on this boating accident, couple of idiots drunk and hitting an orca and in the process one of them breaking their collar bone the other in the cell here.

Well, got a minute to go over today's mind scrambling? He grin,

Brian could always make Sam at ease and in spite of himself he grinned, not funny Bri….but ya, lets grab some dinner and you can fill me in.

They decided to eat by the docks. A ferry was coming in for the last run from Anacortes. The dock was dressed in Christmas finest; lights and wreaths hung from every light pole and the town was pretty much deserted this time of year from tourist. Only locals kept a few shops open, the booths that were open during spring and summer all closed down months ago. The quiet allowed the sounds of waves to be heard echoing across the town center. A light drizzle began to fall as the men walked to the end of the pier. A wave to the boat crew, banter of good barbs to one another, bringing laughter along with sounds of the sea.

Brian stared out to watch the island reef and watched smoke billow from chimneys. Home and heart, he always felt it and it was palpable in the air. This was home; the ache of missing his parents started to trickle into his heart. Christmas was never the same without them and though he is a grown man and glad for the company of Sam, he never had the family connection or belonging to someone ever since they've been gone. In a sense, he was orphaned, maybe that was another connection he had to Nicki as well to Sam. They all wanted to feel they belonged and was needed.

Interrupting his thoughts, Sam said hey...Brian... what's going on inside that head of yours?

He could feel the hint of embarrassment creep over his face being caught in deep reflections and mush of love and loss.

He took his time, found his wit and laughed off the echo of pain that stabbed inside.

Well, I guess we should talk 'bout the session. It really wiped her out Sam.

Sam looked at his brother. He knew, saw the signs of a man drowning in love and didn't know what to do about it. He saw and was concern for the pain his friend might end up feeling.

Brian, we don't know if she's married or not.

Brian snapped at his friend. Don't you know I think of this? But she was hurt Sam and if it was by someone she married I will kill him myself for laying hands on her.

We don't know Brian, we don't know the trouble she ran from or maybe still in. just be careful that's all, be careful

I can't Sam; my head is trying but ….

Ya, Sam said I know.

So, tell me about the session.

Brian recounted the story, the fear, the crying even the joyous moments that Nicki relived. Sam listens carefully and intently. He felt that it was almost his story, and like a bolt of lightning that hit him. Sam was jolted.

Brian, he exclaimed…where did you say she was originally from?

Brian was startled by the intensity of the question, something in the manner and tone Sam asked.

Why? What are you thinking Sam?

It's a hunch but I am feeling like I just got suckered punch and my instincts are never wrong.

With that, Sam said he wanted to see Nicki ASAP, without question, Brian and he went to the car.

The men didn't speak during the drive over. Sam was pensive and stared out the window as Brian drove. Brian didn't like the way Sam looked and his gut began to knot. He replayed over and over in his mind what he might have said, what might have triggered this reaction in his friend.

When they pulled up, they saw Nicki, she was dressed in a long brown sweater, black turtle neck, and jeans tucked inside boots. Her blonde hair loose by her shoulders and she was picking what herbs she had and winter vegetables. His heart thumped inside and he said a silent prayer that whatever brought her to this island it was meant to meet him.

She looked up and waved. She was happy to see them both. They were becoming so important to her and said a silent prayer of thanks that these two strong, dependable upstanding men were in her life. They protected her, and more than that they were her family and friend. She was safe and happy around them without judgment. She knew she must have a checkered past that she was blocking and hoped it wasn't so bad that either Sam or Brian would leave her once it came out to light. She gathered her vegetables; she was making a stew and already had bread baking in the oven. The men got out, Brian waved but Sam had his hands in his pockets. She could see his face and on it she didn't like the look she saw. Her stomach began to turn and she braced herself for what Sam had to say.

Embracing a hug hello they walked silently inside. She went to brew some coffee, checked the bread, anything to keep her hands busy. When she came into the room she found Sam building a fire. Brian sat silently, all three waiting for Sam to speak.

It seem hours but it was just in reality a minute or two before Nicki finally blurted….Ok Sam what is it? You're killing me with the silence.

He looked at her, and for the first time, she felt it was like seeing her for the very first time. He stared inside her eyes and soul. She wanted to flee but didn't, hold her ground for what was to come.

Sam said. Nicki. Do you remember anything more from today's session?

She said bits and pieces of things, images really since I left the doctors. Why?

It's a hunch, and it sounds crazy even in my head, as I replay what I am to say over and over again, but my gut is never wrong …

Sam, my god what what is it she exclaimed.

I think you are my sister.

She stood. Dumbfounded. Lost for words. She didn't even think she breathed.

Brian jumped up…what? Sam what are you saying? How can this be?

Sam was stoic and didn't waver in his voice. I know Brian god I know it sounds nuts, but it's too close to the same story, think about it, the timing, and inside, my gut inside here in my heart, I feel this is true.

She stood there staring at him. Her mind swimming with questions. But the only one that came out was

Wouldn't you know me?

He looked at her. And said, I always thought you looked like my sisters and mother, but you were a baby when I left, when we were taken away from each other.

But I know, it sounds crazy, I just feel it.

She just said, I don't know, I always felt comfortable around you, but I don't remember Sam, I don't.

What if I am not?

Sam said its ok, but let's finds out first

How, she said?

We'll take a DNA test here; I'll call Dr. Simpson and arrange it as soon as possible.

God is all she could say.

Ya, he said …Ya

Well, Brian said…Let's go have some food, I'm starved.

With that they both looked at him, grateful for the distractions and laughed.

Brother, she thought. Could that be why she came to the island?

CHAPTER 14

DNA

The appointment finally came, it 'took weeks before they could get it scheduled and now waiting to get results. The waiting was agony.

Sam was grumpy and snapped a lot at people he worked with. He even avoided Brian and Nicki.

Brian busied getting Christmas shopping done, it was Christmas Eve and Brian hopped the sea plane to go to Seattle. He knew he was going overboard but wanted this to be a good Christmas for Nicki. He bought a few things he saw a snow globe with a tiny silver angel inside; he saw an amethyst stone on a silver chain that caught his eye and felt she had to have it. He bought chocolates and perfume too, gloves and new phone for Sam.

Being done, his phone rang and it was Nicki, she wanted to know if he could be back for dinner. They found themselves talking each day sometimes two or three times a day about nothing at all. They talked at night with chocolate by the fire and becoming more and more friends. They haven't discussed the kiss since that day, it was an awkward secret between them and he felt silly for not broaching the subject with her. Apart of him felt it was fear of her not wanting to be more than friends and fear that she didn't have feelings for him as him her. But he knew he had to deal with this. His heart was full of her, and it wasn't fair to him or to her to continue this way.

She met him at the dock, a big surprise to him and suddenly he was hoping nothing was wrong. But her smile but him immediately at ease. She was there just because, and wanted to surprise him. Brian felt he just got the best gift, unbeknown to her, he smiled and she wanted to know why hey she said why the big old grin

Nothing, he said and gave her a playful bump as they walked, him carrying his armloads of presents.

Sam was to come over that evening, the would open gifts and have dinner and tell stories of Christmas pasts. Brian gave Nicki her gifts and she sighed and squealed at each one. She loved the snow globed and the innocence of her was so overwhelming that it brought tears to Sam's eyes. She made them put the necklace on her and vowed not to take it off. Sam gave her boots of soft brown suede and fur inside, hat and gloves too. She gave Sam a scarf of red, Brian a blue one and both got a silver frame with a picture of her and them inside it. They both loved it!

Sam and Brian told her of their first Christmas as kids in that house and they laughed of the stories of antics they put Brian's parents through. Brian showed her pictures from albums and they drank eggnog and enjoyed the moment of being friends and family. Being so late, Sam decided to stay over; he took Brian's folks room, Brian went to his place and Nicki to hers. She sat and watched the moon. Happy and content, she turned to sleep.

Morning came, Nicki crept to the kitchen it was really still early, she brewed a pot of coffee, opened the curtains to see snow was lightly falling. It delighted her so much that she ran outside to dance trying to catch a snowflake in her mouth. It was so peaceful and she was silly but she knew she was alone and free to enjoy this moment.

Cold, wet from the snow, she went back reluctantly in the house. Being it was Christmas day; she decided to bake fresh homemade cinnamon rolls for Sam and Brian and began to make the dough.

Few hours later, sleepy and groggy the men strolled into the kitchen, the smell of cinnamon rolls made them drool….

OMG cinnamon rolls Sam exclaimed! They both rushed to grab one from the plate. Thick with white icing they slurped in cinnamon heaven,

Bantering and good nature ribbing ensued and they decided to get dress and go to Lime Kiln see if any orcas were out to play.

This delighted Nicki, she raced up the stairs to change Sam's phone rang on his belt. She stopped mid stairs looking down at him. Sadden to the thought he might have to go to work. She watched him he was nodding and suddenly his face went from happy to stern and a bit pale.

I know he said, I know. I haven't the right but I have fallen in l love with you.

She looked down, then up to his face. It was a sweet face she thought. Strong, handsome, kind, tender.

He went on, I know Nicki I know. You cannot love me yet, but I had to tell you. Don't be mad at me.

She smiled, looked at him, reached to touch his face, feeling the stubble, tracing the outline of his lips and leaned in and sweetly kissed him.

Brian, she said. I am in love with you too. But …

He stopped her and kissed her again. Deeply, passionately.

She was dizzy and as he pulled away, he looked at her.

We will be slow. We will wait for you to know who you are. But you will know that I love you and for now that is enough.

Before she could respond, the orcas came up out of the water, big, beautiful with their cubs besides cresting out of the water and splashing back down, it was magnificent! Nothing could be more perfect and in a sense it was a sign of blessing of the kiss given by a wonderful man.

She smiled and closed her eyes again,

Why are you closing your eyes he asked?

Because she said, the best things are unseen, a kiss, a dream, a wish…and with that he kissed her again.

CHAPTER 16

MEMORIES CRASH

She was tired, restless. The wind was up that evening. A storm was heading their way and something was making her edgy and she didn't know what. She heard the trees slap against the windows and with every scrapping sound she jumped a little. Finding that being in the room wasn't any comfort, she decided to go down, brew a cup of chamomile tea. As she made her way down the stairs, the lights went out. Knowing the house the way she did now she wasn't as scared, she held onto the railing and carefully crept downstairs finding her way to the kitchen. She fumbled thru drawers and found matches, feeling her way to the table to light candles she always had out. The kitchen became a glow and was light enough for her to see. The stove was fortunately gas, so she filled the tea pot, set it up on the stove to warm.

The wind was stronger now; a whistle could be heard thru the doors and windows. A shiver ran up her spine yet it wasn't cold in the house. A soft tapping sound came from behind and she jumped as she saw the shadow standing in the glass door panel's .she began to shake until she heard the voice of Brian. Oh thank god she said and opened the door. He stood there, windblown, rain began to fall and he looked worried.

I saw the candle he said, I couldn't sleep either and was concern, so are you alright.

She smiled. Ya, she said. Just a little edgy from the storm I guess. Making tea, want some.

Sure ok, ya and he came inside.

She walked with him behind to the kitchen; the pot began to whistle as she pulled down two mugs.

I was having chamomile…do you want the same?

Sure ok, anything.

As she turned the wind blew harder and a loud crack shook the house

She snapped around as Brian rushed toward the sound.

With that another slam, bang and large branch flew thru the front glass window shattering it to pieces all over the living room floor.

Nicki stood, white as a ghost. Eyes glazed and started to swoon.

Brian turned grabbed her, Nick, Nicki he cried

She turned looked into Brian's eyes and said. I remember. Get Sam.

It took around 20 minutes for Sam to get there. He was half asleep; because of the storm, he was up responding to calls earlier and only gotten to sleep about an hour before Brian's call.

Nicki helped sweep up the broken glass before Sam came, Brian was already placing plywood to cover the hole. They didn't speak, but kept busy. Brian didn't like the way Nicki was so serious, pale and made sure he watched her closely.

Sam watched her dump the last pieces of glass in a trash bag and haul away, he mouth a firm grim expression but made no move to help her. When she was out of the room, he leaned over to Brian and asked?

Don't know, bro he said, the glass shattered and she asked for you, she's been quiet and pale since.

She came into the room, sat down, she was stronger somehow, her movement was purposeful and she asked the men to sit. They faced her and she quietly began to tell her story. She asked if they should record it for Dr. Lane, but both men assured her they wouldn't forget one word she said.

She said she remembered living in a shelter on and off for six months. She hitched a ride for three days and landed in Portland Oregon. She got a job working in a local diner, cooking and waiting tables. She met a man named Steve. He was tall, handsome, and cocky, always came in the place, and ordered her special plate of hash and eggs omelet. Said she was so pretty, said a lot of pretty things. She was flattered. He was older, said he owned a garage, going to have a chain, in reality he was in debt, a thief and a drug dealer. But she didn't know it then, it wasn't until later, when she was entangled with him, he pursued and within a month she moved in with him. That's when the beating started. It was over something silly, something she said, he used a fist and socked her in the stomach, knocking her to the floor, and then always a kick followed. He made her believe she deserved somehow, she wasn't pretty enough, made enough, did enough. She flirted with a customer or that is what he said, and a beating would follow. After a while, it became after he lost a job, account, sale or whatever, she was the bearer of his bad mood.

Sam and Brian didn't move, and then didn't even breathe. They had their hands in fists and they clenched and unclenched. She went on, it was like she was telling a story, it happened to someone else.

She was with him for 5 months, she found she was pregnant. She was devastated and prayed that she wouldn't carry. She knew how that sounded but she was so scared. Steve found out, and for the first time, he was better, softer, he became the man she once remembered. He was nice, loving. Talked to her belly and made plans with her bout new home leaving Portland going to Seattle and having a new life.

She was happy, and within a month or two, they moved to Seattle.

At first it was great. They had an apartment 14th floor, little one room place, had a balcony and Steve could walk to work. At that point it was harder for her to find work being pregnant, so she made cookies and pies, sold from the apartment for extra income.

One day, Steve came home late. He was high. He said he lost his job; he wanted her to pay for him moving there. He brought home men, they gave him money, and she was to be nice to them. She knew what that meant and refused. They raped her anyway. This now became a nightly ritual. One night one man saw her belly and refused. Took his cash back. Steve was enraged and began beating her. He slapped and kicked she began to hemorrhage, it freaked him out he called the ambulance. She lost the baby.

While in the hospital, she told the nurses, but she was scared and weak from the loss of the baby and it all. One nurse told a cop, they came by and spoken to her, but she heard them in the corridor laughing with Steve, he was charming, said she was being crazy and the cop agreed you know how women are…with that she knew there wasn't anything or anywhere she could go.

He took her home, and for a few days he left her alone and she was grateful; she didn't eat she didn't clean or cook. She didn't even care anymore. Then he started again, he began to beat and rape her nightly. He left during the next morning; she did what she needed to do and bravely locked the door. When he returned he was banging and banging yelling for her to open it up. The commotion caused the neighbors to call the cops, as she watches the lights and car pull up, Steve still threatening at the door, she walked to the window and jumped. The glass broke around her as she fell, floating and falling to the street below. She didn't cry out she didn't scream, she could hear people below yelling, but she was just falling and praying it was the end.

The next she knew she was in a hospital, tubes in and out of her. Voices saying she was miracle to be alive. She was there for a month or two, She gotten better, she was healing physically, when she found the strength to start looking up her family, using the computer a nurse let her have to use. That is when she goggled the James in New Jersey, found an old newspaper article about her mother, father, brothers and sisters. She found Sam's name and read him at the island. That is how she came to her. But somewhere, leaving the hospital, she gotten lost, she forgotten her name and memory, the rest you know.

She didn't realize tears where down her face, she saw Sam and Brian and saw shock, anger, horror and tears flowing as well. Sam went to her first, and all he could do was hug her. Hold her tightly and stroke her hair.

We will find him, I promise you, he whispered. He will pay for hurting you.

CHAPTER 17

NICOLAS STEPHEN

He was known as a fast driver, fast talker, lover of women and a mean SOB, that didn't play or fight fair.

Blonde, blue eyes and a dynamic smile. Woman swarmed to be around him, guys wanted just to be noticed with him. He was good looking, even with the scar that ran along his right cheek, remembrance of a fight long ago that cost him 10 stitches.

He was energetic and dynamic, educated but on the streets not with books as he dropped out of school at age 16.

He worked when he wanted, got what he wanted. His passion was fast cars drinking and women and making money the easiest way he could.

Dreams of his youth were driving in Indy 500 but he never seems to make it on the circuit. He was known as good driver but unstable and no one wanted to risk backing him. He had a temper was stating it mildly, he was in and out of detention halls as a child, kicked out of his house by his father by age 13 after being caught setting the pet cat on fire and trying to rape his mother.

He left and never looked back. That was his motto and method, in cause trouble until you get caught and once he couldn't talk his way out of it, he left town.

Moving around, he found his way to Seattle. He stayed here now for 3 yrs. And time was beginning to make him itchy and edgy so moving on was on his mind. Rent was due, and since Megan gone, it was hard to come up with money fast. She was a hot little ticket for him that brought money to him with eager assholes that would pay for humping anything and he charged double for someone as good looking as her.

Stupid bitch, he thought. Cost him a pretty penny and a good little business until she whacked out and jumped from the window.

Now, not only was there rent due and hassles from the landlord,

The cops were around asking questions of the crazy bitch that jumped from his window.

The day she did it, he dodged questions, saying he didn't know her name as they carted her off in the ambulance. But, she must have been talking as they are now coming around more and more.

Packing up, he found clothes of hers and decided to burn them along with the apartment when he left. He continued to fill up his duffle bag, pulling out money he hidden in the closet when pounding at the door from the landlord and cops.

Telling him to open up. He stood quietly not even breathing. In the closet he waited until he heard them leave. Stupid assholes, he said to no one. Not his first rodeo and he was leaving as soon as it hit dark.

He also knew the slimy super would fall asleep with a bottle in his hand as he did every night around 8pm. All he had to do was waiting, and then he would leave and leave a big bon fire to send him off on his way. Pay back the fat bastard that demanded him to pay money for living in a rat hole.

No, he thought, no one going to rip off Steve or Stephan…whatever name he chose to call himself. That was also the beauty of his brilliance; no one ever really knew his real name. He changed it as it suited him and the situation. No, he wasn't stupid and with a slight grin he continued to pack and then pour gas all over the place…

CHAPTER 18

SPRING BRINGS BEGINNINGS

Spring was fast approaching. She was to go by her real name. It was to help her regain her lost memory. It was still foreign and apart of her felt that somehow the name didn't really belong to her. But it was spring, time for new beginnings. A new change at life and perhaps love too. Megan's thoughts were turning to getting a garden ready. She went regularly to see Dr. Robert but he shorten the days of seeing her fearing she would relapse and lose the chance forever to regain her memory fully.

Brian was out on the sea. They spoke regularly via Skype and he would make her laugh of stories of the crew and made her daydream things he seen at different ports He would also worry her when he told her of troubled passengers, and even some pirating that he encountered with his job. She was always surprised how much she missed him and how much she relied on him as well.

She spoke to him of her sessions and goals of hers to plant the garden.

He would listen patiently and give her encouragement when she said she wanted to paint and redo furniture she'd found at the home.

He was so very kind and her heart was full of gratefulness that she found someone liked him. She wanted to take their relationship slow and he was patient there too. He didn't pressure her, but she knew that a man like him wouldn't wait for her forever. She wanted to be whole and be free to open her heart fully and completely with him, but until she knew everything she ran from she couldn't.

She kept remembering more and more about Steve and the baby she lost. She ached inside to the unborn child, said silent prayers that one day; the child will come back to her. Perhaps even to her and Brian? She smiled at the silliness of this thought, their relationship hasn't yet turned intimate yet, but she felt a little giddiness of the thought of having a normal healthy life including sharing her bed with Brian. As soon as she could rid the hauntings of her past, she could begin again. For this, she was also grateful that she didn't need to share a child with Steve and could begin fresh with Brian. The pain of remembering Steve made her shiver and grow cold. The abuse she suffered still lingered way beyond the bruises and broken bones. At times, she could hear his voice or something he said and her stomach would lurch; making it hard to keep from melting into a puddle of fear.

She shook the thoughts of him away, admonished herself for letting herself think of the darkness she was in. She had it good now, great even. She looked around the home she has grown to love.

It was home. It was loving and warm. The sun shone thru the window, warmth across her face reminded her that she was wasting precious day time and she needed to be out tending to the soil. Herbs needed to be planted and with that, she grabbed her hat, gloves and headed out the door.

Hours later, back aching from the digging and turning of soil, the sun began to set. In the distance she heard the familiar engine sound of Sam's car. She was to have dinner with him and talk about going further in finding Steve and pressing charges. She wanted to let it go, she wasn't anything to him and was glad to be gone and hopefully forever out of Steve's mind. But Sam wouldn't let her, and that she knew he was right, but inside she still feared this man that haunted her dreams.

She saw Sam coming towards her. He smiled and waved; such a kind face he had. She was happy to have a brother in her life especially one as sweet, kind and protective as he was. She wanted to speak with him about finding their siblings. She knew it was a subject he wished not to discuss or pursue; she didn't want to hurt him or make him angry, she could see the pain inside his eyes when she approached this before. But he was lonely and in need of them, he still felt responsible for not being able to protect them, him being the oldest. She tried to reason with him that he himself was a child, but there wasn't any way she could free Sam of his pain and guilt. She decided that she would wait for the right moment to talk with him one more time but if that opportunity didn't come, she would speak with Brian and find them herself. Doing gardening always allowed her to work out any problems she had. Smiling, she bent and touched the soil, said a little prayer of thanks and to bless it to hold her seeds and help them grow full and plentiful.

CHAPTER 19

BURN

He was drinking a latte watching the plumes grow higher and higher.

The sounds of glass breaking, sirens blasting made him smile.

He was thinking of that fat bastard super hoping he was stuck in his easy chair panicking to escape his burning building.

Crowds gathered, comments escaping how sad, questions of how this could happen, inside he just wanted to dance and scream stupid people I did this….and laugh while he saw the horror on their stupid faces.

He was beginning to feel super charged, a great mood forming and the desire to find some sweet little ass to make cower in front of him as he uses her and cover her face with his fists and hit until she couldn't feel anymore. The thought of this made him grow hard and he started to scan the crowds to find a willing subject, just at the moment he was to pounce on his next honey, a whiney little voice came up behind him, yelling his name, shaking him from his mood.

Hey, Stephan, been looking for y our man

He turned to see, Charlie, a skinny scrawny dope head that he sometimes used to run errands and gave his leftover women too when he so desired.

What 'a want Charlie. He growled

Hey man, sorry, let me catch my breath, I ran over here, see the fire, man. Charlie started today more but saw the dark look Stephan had on his face. He hung with Stephan for a quick buck or lucky sometimes to get a woman he wouldn't be able to score on his own, but he was scared shitless of him and knew how dark and dangerous he could be.

Hey man, sorry, he whined.

I got a message for you from that dude from that Iranian place.

King who ever.

Steve began to brush Charlie off but the mentioned of King Jordan name stopped him cold.

His interest was piqued. Jordan was a high roller with more cash Steve could have ever dreamed of in his life. He loved fast women, cars and money. He wore diamonds more than any fancy high class rich lady did and was more twisted in his needs than Steve could ever dream of.

What?? Charlie what is it

Hey, Charlie panted, that king's man is looking for you, he wants to offer you big bucks for that skinny Megan chick you had around you.

Bucks? How much? Steve really was interested now.

He said he wanted her for a week, .million smackers! Charlie all but drooled. In his mind if he played his cards right, he might get a buck or two from Steve if he helped him out.

Million? Steve lost his interest in finding someone to lay. He was now truly excited. Money was the ultimate aphrodisiac and to get an easy million by providing one more bitch to his friend, he could all but drool at the thought of easy money.

So when did he want her? He asked playing it cool, like a million dollar offer was nothing.

By next weekend to bring out to the bay, his yacht will be docked in the slip Charlie said with his toothless grin spreading across his face making him look like a thin pumpkin.

Next weekend thought Steve. Million bucks for a bitch he could care less about. But the immediate problem is that he didn't know where she was. It's been a few months since she took a header out of their place. But he wasn't going to let that technicality stop him. He could find her, with the help of the weasel Charlie, he was sure they could find some lame bitch. His only hope was that she didn't mess up her face too much after her header.

Good mood began to spread more inside him, possibilities of what he could spend this money on danced inside his head.

He slapped Charlie on the shoulder, the stench of sleeping in the streets floated in the air from Charlie's clothes and into Steve's nostrils. He all but vomited in his mouth, but again finding Megan was more important and time was starting to tick off quickly. He had seven days to find her.

Best to begin the last place he knew she was, the hospital.

CHAPTER 20

They walked along the streets of the town she was becoming to love.

He waved and introduced her to people passing by. He told her stories of fishermen, store owners, incidents of him and Brian's as kids playing on the streets.

He spoke of Brian's parents as though they were his own, and how much he missed them. He promised to take her to the lavender farm once blooming began and they spoke of future boat rides to watch the orca's up close and personal. It was so wonderful to think of tomorrow and to plan ahead of things to come. To plan a life and have wonderful people to do things with.

He kept things light and causal, watching her from time to time seeing her reaction and smile to the stories he told.

They walked and found a bench to sit at. He didn't want to darken her spirits or the great mood both of them were enjoying but he had to speak of finding Steve.

He told her that he contacted the physician's that was in charge of her care during her stay in the hospital. He used his police status to gain information that they were really reluctant to share. He found the last known address of where she lived and told her he was going to go to Seattle in the morning and doing some inquiring.

She felt her whole body grow cold as ice. No matter how hard she tries to fight it she started to tremble. Tears began to flow and she was so frighten. Please, she whispered, do we really have to?

Sam placed his around her shoulders. Its ok, Megan its ok

I will protect you, and I promise he won't find out I am looking for him, I just need to track him down and I have fellow colleagues at the Seattle PD that will help me apprehend him when the timing is right.

She tried to feel better but every fiber of her being was tingling with fear. He's dangerous she said. I don't remember everything yet, but I know deep inside, that he is more dangerous than we want to acknowledge.

Sam smiled. He knew scum and him even more what to catch him and have him locked up throw away the key.

The sun set, the hues of purple and pink brushed the night sky,

She watched it, tears falling. Gently, Sam took her and steered her to a local café…Let's get some hot chocolate with marshmallows …She looked up to him and just smiled. The knots in her stomach forming tighter and tighter.

Sitting together, Megan tried to busy her mind from the subject of finding Steve. She stared at her marshmallows as they melted into the steaming hot chocolate.

Penny for your thoughts

She looked into his eyes, taken from the deep thoughts that were consuming her. She hesitated for a moment then asked

Tell me about our mother.

Sam blew out a breath. He knew they had to continue to talk about their past, most p art of him wanted to just forget it, bury it with everything and move on. But he guessed she needed to know where she came from in order to move forward.

She was kind. He remembered. She always dressed in pretty dresses even while she cooked and clean. She smelled of lemon polish and Clorox as she was a stickler for keeping everything clean and tidy.

She would sing when she baked. He closed his eyes to bring up the vision of their mother.

She wore her hair in a high bun and I can remember the early mornings when it was just her and him sitting in the kitchen, she baking something and she would pour a cup of coffee one for her and one with a lot of cream for him.

It was their special moment of time together. She would talk of growing up in Italy and how her father was a hard working fisherman that loved the sea and would at times take her to the docks and she could play on the boats.

Megan stared at him as he recalled the moments. The pain of her still resonated on his face. His voice caught at moments as he tried to chase the tears away. Megan tried to visualize what she looked like and the home they all shared. It was hard as she was just too young and nothing came to her.

Sam was beginning to describe the way their mother looked when interrupted by his phone.

Sam here, his voice was a bit raw and he cleared his throat to avoid any detection of pain to the caller.

Instinctively Megan knew something was really very wrong. Sam's whole body went ridged as color of fury crept over his face.

He kept cool as he spoke in short precise answers. He got up and paced around, finally walking outside the restaurant and far from her earshot.

When he finally came in, he gruffly barked her to grab her stuff and they were leaving.

Dread filled her and she started to shake as she grabbed her purse. She didn't ask any questions, she just followed him in quick paces as they hurried to the jeep.

It seemed like hours but it was only minutes before Sam began to speak.

That was my contacts in Seattle he began.

She listen carefully, she wasn't going to interrupt. He said that his former partner was contacted by a drug dealer scum that spent more time in jail his whole life than out, a low life they sometimes used as a snitch to break cases, came to tell him some information about her.

It seems this snitch had a 'friend 'that was bragging to him about a big score, million dollars and he was going to get some of it all if he helped to find you.

There seems to be international dignitary that the feds has their eye on. He lives on a yacht, out of reach for being arrested as he has diplomatic immunity. This scum runs drugs, guns and white slavery. Apparently, he wants you.

She froze. She didn't even think she was breathing. It wasn't real. Her? Million dollars? White slavery? It all seems to far fetch and crazy. She wasn't anybody. She wasn't worth a million dollars, it was absurd.

She started to say so and Sam slammed his breaks grabbed her wrist and with gruffness said…Don't…

Don't underestimate this type of thing. I've seen it, there are cases of missing women and anyone lucky enough to be rescued or escape was messed up forever. It's torture beyond your imagination. This is real this is serious and you're in real very real danger.

She wanted to vomit. Her world began to swim before her eyes and she could only shake.

CHAPTER 21

HUNT BEGINS

Charlie made his way around the back of the alley of the hospital.

He had a buyer that worked inside and he knew if he gave him a nickel bag of coke he would get the information Steve needed.

The wind whistled thru the alley creating a sound. A chill made Charlie involuntary shudder. Cats snooping by the trash cans made for entertainment while Charlie waited. He watched them dig then fight over bones from an old chicken carcass. The bigger one swiped, gave a loud howl, trying to intimidate the smaller one, but the smaller one was quicker and faster as it grabbed the chicken and ran. Yeah, thought Charlie, just like him, he was quicker, smarter and faster, he would out smart Steve and in the end get all the cash himself.

Charlie wrapped his arms around himself, he was anxious and jittery waiting for the dude he only knew as Zee. The coke in his pocket burn with desire for him to take it himself, give him instant courage and strength but he knew he had to get this information on this Megan chick. Steve was waiting, and nothing would stop Steve from beating him senseless or ripping him off when the time came. One problem at a time, Charlie boy, he told himself. Get this and then maybe be friends with Jordan and be a part of his crew. Thoughts of this took Charlie in daydreams of money, women and boats of his own. Going to exotic places and getting respect he so rightly deserved. Yeah, he thought, Steve weighed him down, and he was going to gain bigger and better people that would take him to new heights.

Zee came down the alley, white coat wrinkled and dingy. He wore a skull cap, jeans and white shoes. He was an orderly, nobody really special, which pushed people in wheel chairs and fetched supplies when ordered by fat nurses that were too lazy to do it themselves. Being unknown had its perks he thought, as he could go in and out of places, stole jewelry, cash in bedside tables, had free access to information of patients and some were well known people. He made copies of medical records of the rich and famous, took pictures of them drugged up and sleeping, sold some to local tabloids as well he took medication to sell for quick bucks, all this he has done throughout his year working there and no one was the wiser, they barely even know name. He was a loner, that was ok, this was just a job and that was all he thought about it. He had bigger goals, once he got the cash to move on he was going to California, sun, sand, surf and women. He almost had enough saved. Just a few more months of washing bedpans and mopping floors after puking patients, he was gone, he just had to give up the coke, get clean, and then he would become a surfer. The sun would be his drug of choice. He still had the looks for 25, only a few signs of his drug habit showed on his face and his weight. He would kick it soon he told himself, gain weight, muscles and tan. He smiled at this thought, yeah, he would go.

Charlie watched his score walking up to him. Normally the cash would be what he wanted but this time, the information was good as gold.

Zee gladly took the coke. Free for just going into records and finding out this chick information. This was his lucky day and told Charlie he would have the information by the next day and agreed to meet again same time tomorrow. Charlie smiled, shook Zee's hand and walked away; he called Steve on his way, letting him know that tomorrow they would know where Megan was.

Steve hung up the cell phone. Tomorrow he would meet this junkie himself. Charlie was useful but would be a liability if he knew too much. He was going to rid himself when the timing was right of the little weasel once he had his use of him.

CHAPTER 22

PROTECTION

Sam was on a mission. He set up a mini headquarters at the house. He called in Brian, got him up to speed on the situation. Brian was due to come home later in the day. Sam's old partners were heading there on the afternoon ferry as well as an agent with the FBI.

He had docile on Steve his known accomplices and anything he could find on King Jordan Ali Saad. There wasn't a lot of pictures of either men, Saad was slippery and under watch with the FBI for many years. He couldn't wait to get more of the information once the agent showed up.

Megan was beyond nervous. She barely slept since finding this information out. She watched in silence as Sam played out files, brought in white boards and tacked pictures of Steve and two other men on the board.

She vomited at the sight of him and wished she didn't remember him. She could feel his breath on her neck and at times she could hear his voice whispering her name. She had constant chills and would jump at any noise around her. When she did sleep, she saw his face, staring, grinning, telling her he would take her, she was his, and would do what he commanded of her. Can't run bitch he sneered and she would wake, shaking, cold sweat dripping from her.

She busied herself in her garden; she couldn't find peace there anymore. She felt him watching her, she knew that was crazy but she swore he was there, hiding, lurking in the trees.

She was happy to hear Brian was coming home and went into the kitchen to prepare food for the men that would be over taking her living room.

She made coffee, a casserole and was beginning to bake cookies when Sam walked in. She looked tired, pale and withdrawn. He called her doctors without her knowledge and informed both them of what was happening. They too were concern of her mental status and breaking. They offered to give her some sedatives and he was grateful. He was trying to approach the subject with her.

Look tired honey, he said.

She looked up and gave a grin. I'm fine really, she lied.

Look, Megan, I called Dr. Robert, he said he'd give you something to sleep, I think you should.

No, she shook her head.

I don't want to be in a fog. I need to be alert she said.

No, he started to argue but then knew it was useless trying to. She was stubborn he was beginning to learn, a lot like him.

He won't touch you. I promise he said and went to hug her.

She was stiff, and trembled as he held her.

I know, she said into his shoulder. She held her face against him and just held on to the strength of him.

I'm sorry, she said.

Sorry? What the hell for?

For getting you involved in this. For bringing this onto you. He's dangerous Sam.

Sam smiled. Looked into her face. Look at me he said firmly,

I am not afraid. I am a cop and a damn good one. He isn't going to touch you. I promise you this.

She smiled weakly. The guilt of putting her brother into danger was so much for her. She began to weep.

He let her cry. It seems to be a good release and what she needed. Then she surprised him. She stepped back and wiped her tears. Took a big breath and then she became calm. She looked into his face and then said. No damn it NO

I will not cry. I will not be afraid. I am tired of being afraid of him.

She said with all the courage she could summon.

I am a James. I am not going to give my power to him. I will fight.

With that, he smiled and said, yes you're a James and we don't back down. They began to chuckle, more of the need to release, the laughter felt good and that was how Brian found them, standing there, tears dried on their faces giggling like idiots.

The house was buzzing with people; cell phones ringing, laptops set up on the dining table. Folders, faxes,

pictures all were being reviewed by three men Sam, Brian and Sam's former partner Jimmy Hoffman.

Jimmy a 30 yr. veteran, top of his class, former marine and Green Beret. He commanded the room not only in size but in manner.

He barked orders, asked questions and wanted to 'grill" Megan on all she knew of not only Steve but Jordan Saad.

She barely could speak around Jimmy, not to mention remember the man in question. She tried, but frustrations of blocks in her memory kept her from telling him what he wanted to know.

Sweat would pour off her as she pushed herself to remember, in one moment Brian would get angry and step in to protect her and at times, the heat of the moment, the anxiousness of knowing they needed to catch these men, often fueled tension and bitter words between them all.

Brian called for a break. He wanted to walk with Megan, spend some alone time with her. It was late and they've been going non- stop since he arrived. It was a whirlwind of information, emotions and fear all rolled into desperate need to protect her.

Jimmy conceded to break for the rest of the night and to begin again bright and early in the morning. They all decided it was best to stay in the house making it more convenient to work. Megan made up beds, put out fresh towels for the men and made a mental note to go shopping in the morning to make sure she had enough food for them all.

The FBI agent was to be on the morning ferry, Sam and Jimmy was going to meet boat to get a head start on information.

They all adjourned for the night. Brian lingered behind to help clean up and to spend alone time with Megan.

As she gathered up cups, saucers and putting them in the dishwasher, she started turning off lights, when she stopped and turned to Brian. There weren't words, just a need to be held as he went to wrap his arms around her.

He gently kissed the top of her head and held onto her as tightly as he could, not only for her but for himself as well. He wanted not to let her go; he knew with him, she would be safe.

CHAPTER 23

Z

Zee saw the black SUV as he turned the corner heading back to work. Immediately he knew he was busted. He's been in and out of trouble most of his life, some he talked his way out by becoming a snitch to the local narcs. He wanted to run but knew that was also futile, he would be caught then slammed on the hood of a car, besides he was too wasted to even try.

The men got out of the car, flashed the badge, and told him to stop, hands in the air, down on his knees. He felt the hard cement on his knees, his hands on his head, they were saying something to him but he didn't understand and then suddenly he was pushed to the ground, his face hit the pavement, causing his nose to bleed. He began to laugh, dread was inside him but he was uncontrollable, squealing out a laugh, tears mixed with blood and dirt down his face. He was lead to the back of the sun, cuffed and bleeding, head swimming with cocaine with visions of blurred faces in front of him. That was the last he

remembered as he awoke in a cell. Achy, his mouth feeling he ate cotton; he tried to wake up and get alert. Smells of urine puke and body odor filled the air. Nausea swept over him, he hadn't Zee by the arm as soon as the door opened. Fear and dread curdled in his gut, his mind tried to think what he could have done or knows that this guy might want. A deal was always good and as he tried he couldn't come up with anything. As he was being lead stumbling down the hall, being half walking half dragged trying to keep up with the cop.

His mind was rapidly trying to come up with anything, what next big sale or import of drugs, what heist, killing he might know, he thought and thought then it hit him, a smile began to form.

What's so funny scum? The cop barked

Well, Zee said, I got news for you. It's big too.

Ya, what is it?

Zee proceeded to tell him of the possible kidnapping of Megan, the yacht, white slavery. Once he began to talk it was hours before he stopped. The detective, feverishly writing it all down, Zee knew this was big and he just became more valuable to this yahoo detective.

It was dark by the time he was finished telling all he knew. He was starving, tired and wanting another score. Celebration of getting out of jail free card he so nicely handed to the asshole cops and their bosses.

He was center of attention all day, they hung on every word he said and he relished the limelight. He was asked to wear a wire possibly to catch Steve, the Arab and his contact Charlie. Charlie he felt bad for as he was always good to get the best shit to get high on with the best prices. He agreed to wear a wire in a week. He was going to be important and this would rack up extra "get out of jail" free points he smiled. Ya, it turned out to be a great day as he made his way to find something to celebrate with.

CHAPTER 24

FBI

Sam and Jimmy went to the dock to meet the agent being sent to help them. Jimmy was told it was an expert in white slavery there's an estimate of 50000 men and women kidnapped and trafficked each year into some sort of slavery. Most are never recovered and the odds are staggering on how many victims are lost to foreign land to be horribly abused. The men discussed the facts, figures and severity of this case. Sam didn't like the odds and the situation at all. Not only because it involved his sister, but it hit home another reminder of abuse that women go thru.

The ferry came in; they watched the people shuffle off. Expecting a male agent, they were surprised and embarrassed at their chauvinist mind set when a beautiful lady agent walked towards them.

She was tall, thin, brunette, her hair up in a high pony tail. She wore jeans, boots, blue tee that had FBI on the front underneath a black blazer. She was stunning, and

Sam was speechless for a moment when she reached out her hand to shake his.

Chief James? She asked.

I am agent Sabrina Powers. She smiled as she spoke and Sam's heart began to flutter.

What the hell was wrong with him? He cursed at himself. He was a professional meeting another professional and he mind was acting like a teenage school boy.

He met and worked with beautiful women before, but this one sent his heart immediate fluttering.

He cleared his throat and shook her hand. A shock shot in his hand and she blushed a little, never losing her composure took her hand from his and introduced her to Jimmy.

They left to the house. Sam drove not speaking. Sabrina spoke and asked a million questions of what they knew, filled in information of what they didn't know. By the time the reached Megan, it was clear that their time to avoid danger was dwindling faster than they originally anticipated.

Sabrina had her laptop in her purse. She pulled it out and began to open files; pictures of Arabs under surveillance came up on the screen.

Many were tied to German business men who paid well for the best "cattle" as they were referred to. From there the 'cattle" was sold over and over again to Asians, South America, UK and back to US. It was a larger organization than Sam could dream of. Hard to track them, the 'cattle" was lost and transported to so many areas around the world that the CIA and FBI had informants to help track but even that wasn't fool proof and still many lives were lost.

Sabrina was detached in her mannerism as she described cases, the perpetrators. She was quick, concise, emotionless but very matter of fact. It was as though she was describing a color of paint, Sam thought.

She wanted to meet with Megan. Show pictures of the top leaders of this underworld operation and see if any was familiar. Sam and Brian both started to protest but soon gave in as they knew there wasn't any other way around this in order to save her.

Megan was shown picture after picture. None resonated to her. Sabrina grilled, poked, re asked same questions over and over for nearly 3 hrs. Megan was tired and head was aching. She really couldn't remember, faces began to look the same to her, but Sabrina pushed her on more. Megan felt helpless, useless and began to cry. Brian wanted to step in but Sabrina stopped him.

She was knew the time crunch they were under, she had to push Megan harder, frustration all around the team began to snap at each other. Sam and Brian want to protect Megan, Megan wanting to please and be more helpful just made her feel worse.

Megan fought back the tears but then it was no use, she began to sob and Sabrina abruptly stop speaking in mid-sentence.

She turned to the men in the room, seeing their faces, anger, and helplessness made her take a pause to reevaluate her situation

Ok, she said. Ok Megan. Take a break. Breathe a moment.

She then turned to the men. Ok, All of you outside. Now.

They began to protest, but knew that was useless to do so and with a shrug of defeat, they began to file outside.

Megan began to rise out of the chair but Sabrina pushed her back.

Startled, Megan opened her mouth to say something. But words choked in her throat.

Listen, snapped Sabrina.

I know you're tired, I know your trying, but damn it, it's not enough.

Megan whispered she was sorry, only to be met with Sabrina raising her hands to stop her.

Megan, I am here to help you. This isn't easy, this case, these other women, they didn't have a chance, you do. You have to be stronger, you have to fight. Being weak is allowing this situation and men like Saad, Steve win.

Megan shook her head and said, you don't know, it was horrible, I am not strong, I am scared.

Good, Sabrina said be scared. Be smart, be angry, and be anything but a doormat.

I understand, she continued, and with that she began to unbutton her top three buttons on her blouse. With wide eyes, Megan saw the scars,

Deep and purple, 4 inches long right above her heart. She stared at the scar then at Sabrina's face.

Ya, she said, I know. I was a victim. I know what it's like. I was you, I am you, But the difference, I am stronger now, I fight back this is why I help and do this work. You can too. You already were brave enough to get away with anyway you knew how and you made it to your brother and was brave enough to get your life back.

So It's inside you, you just need to be stronger, Get MAD she said with almost a scream and a plead to Megan.

Megan looked down, took a deep breath. Composed her and wiped away the tears. At that moment something snapped inside. She was Not a VICTIM, that she knew and with all of her will, she looked at Sabrina and asked: teach me to defend myself, to be you. I want to help, I want to win, and I want to catch these men. Help me.

Sabrina cracked a smile, the first since she's been there in this house with these people.

Ok, good. She said. We begin tomorrow. Now, go get a hot shower, tomorrow is a new you, a new beginning and we are going to kick ass!

Megan smiled. Got up, she was a little shaky but wasn't going to wimp out anymore, she silently vowed to be strong and not to cry anymore. She decided to go upstairs, and turned to Sabrina,

Thank you she said. Thank you.

CHAPTER 25

PLAN

Hours, days, turned into a week. Nonstop they met in the living room now dubbed headquarters. Megan would train at night with Sabrina learning self-defense, baked and garden during her breaks with meeting with the team and reviewing pictures.

On Sam insistence she met with Robert to ensure she wasn't taxing herself to much. He and Brian fretted that she would slip back and lose every memory, but Megan felt stronger somehow, more confident, less that fragile bird she was. She felt empowered. She had a mission to beat the men that wanted to destroy her. She wasn't going to allow Steve to take her and abuse her again; she would fight with all she had. Like Sabrina was teaching her it wasn't enough to fight but also to be smart, confident, to think in dangerous situation, keep your wits she said, that will be the edge she would need if anything did happen.

They learned the police information Zee was meeting with Steve and his accomplice in the next few days. Police set up surveillance and microphones to capture everything Steve might say. Mostly, they were hoping he would lead them to the yacht and Saad.

The hum of the anxiousness was all around them. Sam checked in with her time and again to make sure she was ok, reminding her that she wasn't alone and nothing was going to happen to her. But Megan knew that no matter how much they were trying to protect her, something might happen, and that she had to prepare herself for.

Brian and she stayed up late most nights, speaking, talking of futures and plans to explore their relationship further. He spoke of "courting" that made her giggle but it also gave her hope of a tomorrow and putting all of this behind them, she would be whole and able to give herself, heart mind body soul to him. She did love him, and at times sad that she wasn't able to show it like she wanted to.

He was patient, kind, loving, supportive and most of all she knew she could trust him completely. She was now wanting this week to be done, one way or another, she wanted Steve caught and to begin again.

CHAPTER 26

FIGHTING BACK

The days past fast and furious, arguments, plans, and details of the yacht came in minute by minute. Survaliencce equipment tested, planted on the boat by undercover men working as dock hands. Communication with the Seattle PD and Sam's team came in daily. They were to meet with Zee and hook him up with a wire. He was to meet with Charlie and Steve, score some more coke and get them to talk about Megan later on that evening.

Everything was going to plan. Sabrina, Sam, Jimmy and Brian went thru it all movement by movement on how they were to follow, capture both Steve and the members on the boat.

Megan most days just listen. She practiced her self-defense and kept praying that this will be all over sooner rather than later.

The tension in the air was palpable everyone knew what was at stake, news from Sabrina's team informed them of at least three more women was on that yacht taken from Asia, Africa and Ireland. Saad's been busy, Sabrina said. Wondering why and who these women were to be sold to. Even more that was nagging her was why the attraction to Megan. She was beautiful no doubt but there has to be more, it didn't feel right inside her gut, and she's learn to trust her intuition. She's becoming to like Megan, a little sister she's never had, she didn't feel Megan to be dishonest or evil enough to be working with Saad, but there was definitely something she knew or saw that she isn't remembering but Saad wants her out of the way. This puts her more into danger as it will not be just Steve to worry about, Saad was smart and wouldn't leave the task to grabbing Megan just to him alone and would have a backup plan. This is what she needed to discuss with Sam

Sabrina found Sam discussing something heated on the phone. She watched him as he grimaced and clinch his fists. He has a nice face she thought, she admired how he had self-control and was so kind to his sister. His love for her shown thru his actions and mannerisms, and she prayed that he would remain focused when the time came to save her.

Sam abruptly hung up his phone and rushed past her. He didn't see her standing waiting for him and she immediately followed. She knew it was bad news and he would want to discuss it in front of everyone.

Brian and Jimmy were working on video surveillance when Sam came in. They looked up and saw his face and stopped what they were doing.

What's up? Brian asked

Sam just replied with "Zee's dead".

What they all said at once... How???

Found overdosed in the alley by the hospital. PD looking into it for foul play.

Damn, Brian exclaimed. Now what.

No one saw Megan standing nearby and listening. She knew what this meant to the capturing of Steve and Saad, also to free those poor women that were held on that yacht.

Before Sam could respond, Megan spoke.

I will do it. I need to be the one to do this. They all looked at her.

Like Hell, Brian said

No way, Sam chimed in, we will find another way.

No, Megan said sternly. It's me they want. It's logical I can get on board that yacht and help those women.

You don't know if they will drug you and you will be helpless and cannot do anything then it's a rescue mission for three! Exclaimed Brian.

Jimmy and Sabrina looked at each other. They knew this was the best idea. Dangerous yes, but the best plausible plan. They could wire her, they would be close by and to apprehend before the boat left the dock.

They all began to speak at once and arguments ensued. But in the end they all agreed, Megan would be the best choice. Brian was still angry and couldn't agree to this and stormed out of the house.

Megan followed him to reason.

Look Brian, stop walking and talk to me

Brian stopped, he was pissed. Look Honey, don't follow me right now, I'd don't want to talk, I am too mad to speak right now.

Yes, you will. Look at me Brian.

I am not going to let you storm off we need to talk about this.

What are you thinking he said? This isn't a game. He they are dangerous.

He grabbed her shoulders. And wanted to shake her but only could hang on and hug her close to him.

I can't be sure you'll be safe he said. I don't want to lose you.

She spoke softly in his shoulder. I know she said.

I am scared. But this is the right thing to do. I will never be safe with them out there, waiting each day they might come and hurt me. If they don't this time there will be another time. Another day, I can't live looking over my shoulder waiting. We can't live like this.

He stopped and looked at her face and gently kissed her. For a moment they just clung onto each other. Deep in kiss of desperation a d connection. Nothing else matter. At that moment, it was just them and feeling of their hearts beating.

Brian pulled back, lifted her chin and stared into her eyes. Megan he said, I won't lose you. I don't agree with this, but I understand.

I will be there to watch out for you and I won't let them take you. I won't! When this is done, you and I will finish this and be together. I love you Megan that I am sure of and I want a life with you.

She smiled and all she said was I love you to.

With that, he took her hand and walked back into the house. They had a lot to do in a short amount of time. And now the stakes were even higher and the planning had to be précised.

CHAPTER 27

FINAL PLANS

Sabrina worked on holding, firing and concealing a weapon with Megan. During the sessions, she asked questions about Steve and Saad. She probed further making Megan think of the relationship she had and what the link to her is.

Megan shook her head and said she really didn't remember him and she can't think of why they want her. She was a foolish girl that didn't feel confident about her and fell for the first guy that paid attention to her. Sabrina wasn't so sure about this. She knew Megan was vulnerable but she felt that Megan knew more, and inside it was buried and perhaps she was blocking it out or it was truly lost forever but Megan had something Saad wanted and they needed to know before she was to be wired and put in front of him. That knowledge was the key to his capture and to her safety.

Sabrina met with Sam and discussed this with him. He agreed reluctantly that perhaps Megan buried something so horrendous and sadly was the reason Saad was willing to pay big money to have her kidnapped. They decided that Robert was needed to take Megan under hypnosis again, to bring out what was hidden.

They called Robert and he agreed to come over and take Megan under. It was against his better judgment as a clinician but knew the severity of the situation and that timing was of the essence.

The sun began to set; Megan sat outside and watched her flowers close up their little heads for evening slumber. She took in the fragrance of the lavender and rosemary, inhaling it deeply, it calmed her, centered her. She knew she needed to be hypnotized and she wanted to help everyone she really did, but she didn't feel she knew anything, how could she? Was she mixed up with these awful men doing awful things? She had to believe she didn't. This whole mess was so overwhelming at times didn't feel real. She wished she could go back into time and be at that diner, and when Steve flirted she ignored him. How her life would be so different. Brian told her things happened to lead her to him and find Sam, that thought was so pleasant and beautiful but reality lingers she was with a horrible evil man and whatever he did with these other evil men she was wrapped into it. Would Brian still want her afterwards? She worried about that. But one thing at a time. She had to help Sabrina, Sam, Jimmy, Brian and those women held against their will. Whatever happened to her didn't matter more than them.

She was willing to sacrifice her life for theirs. She had the peace of knowing she found her brother and someone that truly loved her unconditionally and that was enough.

She held the lavender a little longer. Said a prayer and sprinkled the blooms around her. She got up and went in to be put under. Fear, tiredness and the unknown weighed heavily on her shoulders.

One, Two Three....ok Megan you are in a safe place. You are being guided to go back and open up to tell us about Saad Jordan.

Take us to the place you met him. Do you understand?

Uh huh she said.

Good, Robert said. His voice calm, soft and soothing.

Now, what do you see Megan,

I see a boat, it's really big. White. It's dark outside.

Good good, he said, tell me more. What's on the boat?

Letters and numbers. N853M she said.

There's a name on it too. She said. Crystal Bay she said

Good you're doing good Megan. Now tell me what's inside the boat

Lots of lights she said. Red and Blue flashing, loud loud music

There are women dancing around a bunch of men.

Who are these men Megan?

I don't ...don't know, no I don't want to say, she cried.

Shh its ok Megan you're safe. Let's forget the men ok, now tell me what else do you see?

She quieted for a moment.

Urge her said Sabrina.

Robert looked at her sharply, Do not interrupt, he scolded.

For a moment, Megan was so still. Then she started to speak.

I am down stairs; there is a room with a big bed and pillows of purple, green and red. There is a man talking to another man. One is Saad he is arguing with this other man. The other man is tall, dark hair with a British accent. He is saying he wanted four women not three. He was saying the shipment of cocaine wasn't there and wanted it delivered in exchange for the guns he shipped to Saad. Said he was the officer of the prime minister and wouldn't be messed with. Then a shot rang out. The British man slumped to the floor. She gasped, Saad turned he didn't know she was there, NOOOOOOOOOOOOOOOOO she screamed; he slammed her against a wall. She hit her head. The room is dark now.

Brian, Sam, Sabrina and Jimmy stared at her. More than they thought. No wonder she was wanted. She witnessed a murder to an official and a link to him, guns and cocaine not to mention white slavery.

Wow, is all they could say at once. Robert guided her back to the present. She was white and pale, starting to shake. Brian rushed to her and took her upstairs to lie down. This was a lot for anyone and now they have more to deal with now.

CHAPTER 28

MILLION DOLLAR PRIZE

Steve heard Zee babble after giving him some prize coke to snort.

Stupid drug addicts are always good to count on to want to use and to spill their guts of what they know.

He was pissed to learn how much Charlie had told him but he would deal with Charlie later. Right now it was learning that the feds knew of Megan being snatched. He also learned where she was, that was more valuable. So he knew he had to deal with feds watching her, but he could get around that and he wasn't going to let some low life crack head mess up his million dollar prize, so as he babbled on and on, Steve reached up behind him, grabbed his neck and stuck a needle full of heroin in his jugular. A mixture of cocaine and heroin would kill him quickly and no one would even waste time on investigating. As for Charlie, he would never see the end of the week.

Steve watched Zee twitch and then die on the side walk; stepping over him he headed to charter a flight to the islands. Megan was there and a place that wasn't that big he would be able to get her and back to the hands of Jordan and his cool million in his pocket. He was all giddy knowing by end of the night he was going to be a millionaire!

He punched the numbers to Jordan, he told him to expect the package at midnight, and hung up the phone.

The flight took less than 30 minutes to the docks of Friday Harbor. He stepped off with all the other loser tourists chatting about their sight-seeing this or that. His mission was to find her and to go. He went to the docks to find a dingy to rent for the next few days. It wouldn't draw attention to anyone for a boat to be out for a few days, romantic evening with his new bride he told the guy. Little touchy feeling with the misses he said with a wink, and the man chuckled and told of days with his love of his life too. Ya whatever Steve thought and smiled and nodded like he gave a damn.

The next step was the hiding of the boat in an area it wouldn't be noticed. He saw a cove with trees low enough to hide without drawing attention and easier access. He looked in his bag and made sure he had a syringe full of heroine to drug her up and make it easier to deal with her. It would be Jordan's problem to make sure she comes down off the high he was about to give her.

He went to the local stores looking for dumb women that would easily chat with him and perhaps spill whatever information on Megan's residence. Wouldn't be too hard in a town this size to know a woman that is mentally unstable that has FBI hanging around. Knowing Megan like he did she was probably in a ball quivering and bawling like she did so many times with him. The bravest thing she ever did was jump out the window but even that she screwed up and didn't die. Right now that was fortunate for him but it won't be of her.

He went to three stores until he found one little blonde giving him the eye and sweet smile. On a normal day, he would have tapped that fine ass, but today he was to remain focus and get his hands on his money. It took less than 5 minutes and a cute little pout from her to know where Megan was staying. Seems like the slut found her a knight in shining armor as a cop to watch over her. No biggie, just one more obstacle and a pig to shoot if need be.

He found her house in 20 minutes. It seemed quiet enough and not a lot of activity likes cars and Feds hanging around. For him, that was excellent. He hiked up a trail near the house and sat among the trees and waited til it got dark. His plan as he watched it in his head was to pick the lock, find her, shoot her up and drag her out. It would take 20 min or so to get to the boat then another 50 or so minutes to get to the yacht. Bing BANG BOOM he said….just like that he was in the money!!!. He had a few hours left until darkness so he called Charlie, told him to head over, catch the ferry and where to meet him.

Just in case he needed help he thought, cover the bases.

Charlie showed up just when the sun was beginning to set. Steve's legs were getting tingling from all that sitting still watching the home. He saw two men come and go from the house. Bitch he thought probably was making some extra cash, guess she did learn from him after all.

Another women tall, pretty brunette came outside and walked around. She was doing some stretches and as she reached up, Steve spotted the gun tucked neatly in her waist band. Oh, this must be the FED he smiled. She was going to be easy to take down. This night was getting better and better he said.

Darkness came; Charlie and Steve made their way to the house. They crept as quiet as they could. They decided to go around the back to gain access. The house was dark and very very still; Steve thought how easy this was. She was always very dumb. This was like taking candy from a baby he whispered to Charlie. Charlie smiled the toothless grin and twitched holding in a snicker. He was so glad Steve wasn't mad at him for Zee and still was going to cut him in on the million deals. What a good buddy he thought, he and Steve will rule the world, so lucky he was with him.

They crept the stairs without any problems, tried the handle of the door and found it open easily. Oh their luck they almost did a dance right there and then. The door opened without any hitch and they both stepped inside. Neither brought a flashlight so they felt their way around the walls until finding a switch as they flipped it on they turned in time to see a barrel pointed at him. Sabrina and Jimmy were waiting, guns pointed at their heads. Steve reached for his and with flash fires rang out and vibrated the room.

Megan and Sam were down on the stairs and watched as Jimmy, Sabrina, Steve and Charlie reached for guns and fired at each other.

It was Megan that fired the fatal shot. She stood took aim and found herself squeezing the trigger, Steve saw her and in his amazement he saw her shoot him as he fell to the ground. Charlie dropped the gun and fell to his knees crying out not to shoot him, Sabrina had him cuffed and pulling up to sit him on the chair to begin interrogating as Steve rolled and shook on the ground. He was bleeding but it wasn't fatal. Jimmy cuffed him and called for ambulance. Megan stood on the stairwell, gun still pointed and frozen into place.

Sam reached over to her, laid his hand on her arm. Put it down honey he said. Its ok put it down.

She heard him; like in a fog she heard him speaking to her and turned to him. He gently took the gun from her as she slid down and plopped on the stairs.

Steve was screaming and wanting a lawyer, threating lawsuits and babbling more nonsense as he was carted off under FBI and police custody. He was shot in the right shoulder under the clavicles and was more shocked that Megan did it. He didn't think she had it in her.

They took his phone, cuffed him, treated his wounds and had him stitched up then to be whisked off to an unknown location to undergo further interrogation.

Charlie on the other hand was talking. And he wouldn't stop. He gave the exact location, time to meet Jordan and what the signal was. He knew who was on the boat to wait for Megan, the other women were from Steve too from months ago, and what happened to Zee. Steve now was facing trafficking, drug dealing and murder.

The problem now was to capture the men on the yacht and to rescue the women on it.

Megan still wanted to go but Sam, Sabrina wouldn't let her. They were fortunate enough that the man at the dingy rental gave Sam a heads up and they were able to make a plan to capture Steve trying to get her. Now, they were going to have Sabrina pose as Megan. She donned a blonde wig, they were of same height and build and in a distance if she kept her head down, it would fool Saad enough to get her inside. Jimmy was posing as Steve, in their mind they never really met just phone transactions and per Charlie if his information is correct, this was to be true. He could go on board with Sabrina and with the undercover feds already in place on the dock, they could apprehend them all.

Darkness was their friend to pull this off. In the dark and distance it would look like Steve in a boat with Megan. They pulled up alongside the yacht flashed a flash light in three bursts, signaling Jordan and his men that they were there and all is a go.

The yacht flashed back, and the dingy pulled slowly nearer to allow boarding. The fog was already rolling in so the mist and darkness provided the shield they needed. Head down, Sabrina radioed the others that she was in place and once on deck they were to storm in.

She pulled a jacket around her, gun in the pocket cocked and ready to shoot. Jimmy was ready to go to, as he steered expertly around the side of the yacht keeping view of them just far enough away so that they would have trouble making out her face.

The ladder down, he climbed up first, Jordan's men there saying things in their language as Sabrina flashed her legs in a short skirt and made her way up to Jimmy and the deck.

Jordan stood in the doorway, smiling. The last witness to his killing is on board and after he had his way with her se would be disposed of along with the sniffling Steve. He had what he wanted and it didn't cost him a dime.

He went below deck, instructed his men to bring the wench to him once she was on board, and to rid the man with her. Take the boat out to sea and to start up the boats. The sooner they were gone from this god forsaken place the better.

The other men had the girls beaten and now passed out. They had their fun with them and they lay motionless on the floor. Alcohol was abundant and they were all tipsy and ready to pass out to sated ready for more action in a few hours.

He undressed and patted his stomach as he watched himself in the mirror. He was getting flabby and would need to start to get into shape. Too much of this American fatty foods and would need to go home for his own kind of food, wine and culture. Too much American was too much he thought and went to lay on his bed ready for the blonde witch to be brought to him.

He closed his eyes, resting for a moment, when he heard shots ringing and vibrating the hull. He dropped to the floor, looking for a robe to cover him and where he left his own gun.

As he turned the door burst open and lights, guns pointed at his face.

FBI they cried out as they rushed him, down on the ground, spread your arms and legs.

Diplomatic immunity he screamed as they cuffed him.

Not today buddy she said and slapped the cuffs extra tight as he was yanked up naked and helpless. Get him a robe she said as two big men grabbed his arms and dragged him to the deck of the boat.

The ordeal lasted 5 minutes. They arrested 4 foreign diplomats, 6 deck hands, the captain, and Jordan. They found an arsenal of guns, drugs and four women of various ages that were beaten, drugged and kept on this boat for months. Sabrina called Sam as soon as it was over. Relief overwhelmed Sam as he thanked Sabrina profusely and hugged Megan for at least an hour. Megan was so grateful she fell to her knees and gave a prayer of thanks to the almighty above, the angels that watched over her and to her mother, that inside she was sure was watching over her.

CHAPTER 29

CLOSURE

It's been six months since the capture of Saad Jordan, Steve, Charlie and the other six men aboard the yacht. Steve was sentence to 120 years in prison for kidnapping, human trafficking, drug dealing and murder of Zee. Charlie made a plea deal and was sentence to 24years and available for parole in 10 years. Saad Jordan has diplomatic immunity and not being cooperative on giving up his national accomplices. However he is being held for questioning and dealing with the government of his deportation and possible imprisonment. Sabrina, Sam, Jimmy still working together to clean up the reports, mess and making sure the hostage women got home to t their families and find their knowledge of any other women they can possibly find. The hours grueling but so far they've put together a comprehensive list of possible locations of missing women long be thought to have died by their families.

Megan and Brian decided to take some much needed time to get to know each other properly. They began their dating and romance ensued. Free from fear and the horrible nightmares that has haunted her for months. Brian wanted to take her to Hawaii to escape all the memories and bask in the sun on the beach, but Megan didn't want to go. She wanted her home return to back to normal no more charts, computers, printouts of Jordan, Steve etc. she wanted her garden and plant new flowers. Bake, clean and be normal.

Reluctantly, Brian agreed. He watched her closely, met with Robert to make sure she was ok and if she would experience any setbacks. Robert assured him that although possible, he felt it unlikely. Megan seemed to be stronger, grown a lot in confidence and taken back her power she lost so long ago to the horrors of Steve.

Imprisoning Steve freed her. Brian was happy to hear this and he said he would always worry bit about this ordeal, he was grateful to have it behind both of them.

On a bright summer morning, Sam and Brian announced they were going over to Seattle to close out some things with the PD and other business. Sabrina was planning to leave in a day or two and Megan wanted to throw a nice dinner party to thank her and Jimmy for all they have done for her.

She gave a nice list of supplies for Brian to pick up for her while in Seattle, she decided to bake a six layer chocolate gaunche cake, steaks on the grill, corn on the cob, large bowl of potato salad and all outside on the bar-b-que. Pit Brian dug the day before. Beer, wine and fun was definitely in order. Pit hot and ready for steaks, music playing everyone in joyous mood. Sam invited the PD team that also helped in Seattle to come over, Megan insisted Sabrina have the remaining team of FBI agents be there as well. She dressed in a light blue summer dress, bare foot and happier than she's been all her life.

Sam had music blaring and grabbed her to dance on the grass; she threw back her head and laughed at his attempt to twist or something

Gyrating to the beat. At one [point Sam grabbed Sabrina and they did some sort of spin that made everyone clap and laugh along with them.

Beer in hand Brian watched it all. How normal and right it felt. In his parents' home that once shared wonderful memories of his own parents dancing and laughing to have it back was homage to them.

He looked to the heavens and raised his bottle, to you mom and dad he said. Then he walked over to Megan, Knelt before her and in front of friends, he proposed. He produced a beautiful silver ring with a blue topaz diamond. It was perfect! Megan was so moved, thrilled and full of love for him she didn't even hesitate and accepted immediately,

Everyone in agreement cheered, Sam hugged him and then her, how perfect his family is he thought and with a small twitch of pang, he thought of his own mother, he other sisters and brother so long ago lost.

CHAPTER 30

WEDDING DAY

Brian and Megan's wedding day was finally here. They didn't want to have a long engagement and immediately made plans to marry New Year's Eve. They felt the joy of the season and beginning a new life together on a new year was good luck. They were putting last year behind them and looking forward to a bright new life together. They decided to marry in an outside ceremony at the light house in lime kiln. Since this was the first place they said their love for each other.

The light house was decorated in twinkling white lights, dozens of bushels of white roses, lavender and white ribbons; They lined the makeshift aisle in white wooden folding chairs adorn in white ribbons with sprigs of lavender. On the ground there was a path of white petals and candles to light her way to the alter.

It was chilly as it was threatening to snow later on. But Megan felt it was perfect. She decided to forego the traditional white gown and chose an ice blue long dress that matched her blue topaz ring. Her hair was swept up in a soft bun with baby's breath and lavender woven in.

She asked Sabrina to stand for her as matron of honor. Sabrina was touched and honored; Sabrina chose a dress of darker lapis blue to compliment the lighter shade that Megan wore. Sam and Brian both wore black suits with blue ties and pocket squares that matched the lapis blue of Sabrina's dress.

Megan didn't want a bouquet; instead as she walked the aisle, Brian held one perfect rose for her to have.

The music softly played, friends she became to know and love stood as she walked towards her love. The snow began to fall softly and gently, encompassing Megan like a soft veil.

Brian smiled as one single tear trickled down his cheek. Sam walked her to meet Brian He was so honored that both his sister and best friend that he felt as a brother were being married. He was so caught up in emotions; he allowed the tears to flow down his face.

Megan stopped mid aisle and brushed the tears from her brother's cheeks. She gave him a hug and continued onward to Brains waiting hands. They started their own vows and Megan looked at Brian her heart full and felt so complete. She said to him once she was lost, now she found her brother, her family, strength to overcome any obstacles, she found a new friend and best of all, she found the love of her life. Once lost now loved. And gently kissed him. Tears flowed as they were pronounced man and wife. During the clapping, Brian stopped and said to Megan and Sam; I have a gift for you both.

Sam and Megan looked perplexed and then Brian pointed. There at the end of the Aisle stood two women and a man. Smiling and holding hands. Sam stared at Brian he had no idea what to make of this.

Sam, Brian said, that is the rest of your family.

Printed in the United States
By Bookmasters